NOTES FROM
THE AFTERLIFE

for Carl and Kathy

with warmest wishes.

Edward
and after ego,
J + L

NOTES
FROM THE
AFTERLIFE

Edward Packard

for Amy, David, Sam,
Chris, Eddie, and Jessica

INTRODUCTION

The day after Jack Treadwell died his lawyer called me and said that Jack had named me literary executor of a book he'd been writing. We had roomed together in college, but I hadn't seen him in years, so I couldn't imagine why he chose me. Maybe he thought I would find it instructive. Anyway, I told the lawyer to send me the book and I'd look it over. It arrived in electronic form the same day. I opened it and nearly laughed as I read the title, *Memoir of My Afterlife*, but that evening I dipped into it and found it so engaging that I thought maybe it should be published. An acquaintance of mine, Charlie Wickersham, is a literary agent, so I called him and asked if he'd take a look at it. "Sure, send it over," he said, "but don't be surprised if I only read a paragraph or two. It's one in a zillion this kind of thing would interest a publisher."

I thought Charlie would never get around to reading even a paragraph, but about six weeks later I got this email from him.

> I read 20 or so pages of MEMOIR OF MY AFTER-LIFE, and I actually enjoyed them. I'm not willing to believe this is a true account of Jack Treadwell's experience in the afterlife, but he is a lucid and provocative

writer. If the book market was not so fraught as it is, it's not inconceivable that some publisher or other might take this on. The downside is that the search for such a publisher would probably require more time than I have available. I think the best course—one in which you'd be amply discharging your duty as a literary executor— would be to self-publish it.

CHARLIE HAVING MADE his pronouncement, I set about following his advice, first reading Jack's manuscript with some care. His title, *Memoir of My Afterlife*, struck me as a bit pretentious. For that reason and because in two places he referred to his work as "notes," I changed the title of this volume to *Notes from the Afterlife*. I think that would have been all right with Jack.

As for the writing, it feels hurried to me in some places, which is not surprising, since Jack was in a perilous state of health when he wrote it and may have sensed that he had little time to live. Even so, I think his book is a remarkable document. I, for one, found plenty to think about in it, and I admit I was intrigued by the circumstances under which Jack wrote it.

Although I don't for a moment think he could have come back from the dead to write a memoir, I can't get it out of my mind that his physician, Dr. Sylvia Kapp, told me that he was propped up in bed, typing on his laptop almost at the very moment of his death, and that he had previously had what she called a "near death" experience in the hospice. Best as I understand it, the term refers to an episode in which the patient has a powerful apprehension of imminent death, which can let loose a flood of emotions and in some cases produce ecstatic behavior; the brain may be flooded with neurotransmitters, like dopamine, that can produce hallucinations and precipitate a heightened state of consciousness.

Jack was near death indeed. The nurse on duty thought he had expired. The hospice doctor pronounced him dead, only to be called back a few minutes later when an aide noticed he was breathing. Dr. Kapp told me that the episode was incident to a remission in Jack's cancer so extraordinary that she subsequently described it in a medical journal. Unfortunately his recovery was short-lived. He died suddenly four months later.

Occasionally one reads of a devout person who has the illusion of having visited heaven. Jack was far from devout. In his later years he had become an outright atheist, so it was remarkable that he chose to write about heaven, and even more so that he imagined he had been there.

Jack loved poetry. He began his "memoir" with a poem and evidently planned to end it with another. Though he wasn't able to complete his work, he had copied a poem to serve as the final page. I retained it, along with the opening poem, in this edition. In several instances he quoted from a literary work without noting the source. I identified these in an endnote.

Edward Packard
Springs, New York

Memoir of My Afterlife

a true account

by

Jack Treadwell

I went to heaven,—
'Twas a small town,
Lit with a ruby,
Lathed with down.
Stiller than the fields
At the full dew,
Beautiful as pictures
No man drew.
People like the moth,
Of mechlin, frames,
Duties of gossamer,
And eider names.
Almost contented
I could be
'Mong such unique
Society.

— EMILY DICKINSON

1

A few days after my eightieth birthday, diagnosed with an inoperable malignant brain tumor and still dispirited by the passing of my wife a year earlier, I contrived to transfer my residence from Arcadia Retirement Estates, Assisted Living Unit 2, to the Burnside Memorial Hospice. Apart from profound weakness, which had been my normal state of being for several weeks, I was suffering from little more than a persistent headache and periods of confusion. Otherwise, the offending carcinoma had not affected my cognitive functions, such as they were. In compliance with my standing end-of-life instructions, which I emphatically confirmed to Dr. Sylvia Kapp, my personal physician, she placed me on a morphine drip—prematurely, you might say, since I was not in severe pain, and my heart, unaware that it had been given leave to quit, was still beating with stubborn regularity. To my great relief, if not delight, Dr. Kapp had been of a mind to conspire with me, or so I thought, in accelerating the process of my demise, for which I rewarded her with a last grateful smile as I felt myself levitating to the vicinity of the ceiling.

I was neither hopeful nor despairing; my mood was one of melancholy tinged with remorse over my transgressions in life, albeit most of them perpetrated at a much younger age. Still, what difference does it make what age we're talking about? I had hurt people and been foolish and indolent, and to tell the truth self-destructive, throwing away opportunities, drifting, almost deranged at times. Now it didn't matter, except that the consequences of what I did and failed to do were still affecting people I cared about, though not enough at the time. But to get on with my dying: Light perceived through my closed eyes varied in intensity, annoyingly. Attendants and nurses drifted in and out: "In the room the women come and go." I was aware of their grave, muffled voices. I glimpsed them through half-open eyes, moving shadows in the muted light, incorporeal, it seemed, and non-temporal, for I had no sense of the passage of time.

Nor had I a sense of how much time elapsed between when I was in this last living state and when my eyes opened and I found myself surrounded by a delicate shade of blue that seemed wholly removed from earthly context. It didn't occur to me that I might be dreaming or hallucinating. Rather, I assumed that I had died and must be in heaven, then just as quickly that this thought was preposterous. For one thing, I had been an agnostic from early adolescence through late middle age, and in recent years an outright atheist: I "knew" heaven did not exist. For another, even if I had been wrong and heaven was a reality, it was highly unlikely that I would be admitted.

But it was heaven I began to imagine I was in, if only because I seemed to be standing on a rug-sized cloudlet in a sea of them extending as far as I could tell above, around, and below me. Perched on some of the closer ones were phantasmal forms resembling human figures. I looked in vain for a point of reference, a way to get my bearings. I tried to walk and had no difficulty taking what seemed to be slow-motion steps.

Strangely, my cloudlet moved with me. Though my body seemed indistinct, as if only its vague form had been preserved, I felt relatively youthful and lithe, and neither besieged by pain nor drugged.

To my astonishment there sounded a long clear blast of a brass instrument. Imagine such a welcome! There he was! Who else could it be but the angel Gabriel, his wings folded neatly over his white cape, the lower part of which flared behind him as if he were facing into a strong breeze, which surely he was not. His horn appeared to be fashioned out of pure gold, but that too would be impossible, since everything in heaven is immaterial. This did not present a problem for Gabriel. He played a series of tones of absolute clarity and purity, an exquisite variation on a familiar melody, a delight to the senses I would not have thought possible. Was it true, as I guessed at the time, that he had played Copland's *Fanfare for the Common Man?* I wasn't sure, but that's what I thought it was, and that Copland may have been divinely inspired when he composed it, in which case, though Gabriel derived this musical flourish from Copland, Copland derived it from God!

I was thinking dreamily along these lines when there appeared before me an incorporeal shape, a shadowy figure barely differing from those I had glimpsed through half-open eyes coming and going in my room in the hospice. I felt an impulse to bow down to this presumably divine figure, but restrained myself, or more precisely, some inner instinct, stronger than my will, restrained me.

Disjointed words formed in my mind: Who, what, you, I? Yet I was not sure that there was a "you," or even that there was an "I," at least not beyond a cohesive feeling of absence of pain and of any impediment to movement. To the extent there *was* an "I," it (I) could only be silent, comporting with boundless space in all directions. Nonetheless, I felt an inexplicable sense of familiarity in my circumstances, and I was not surprised when I became aware of thoughts emanating from the semblance of a human figure before me, though they were not expressed in spoken words; they simply entered my consciousness. Instead of speaking, this heavenly being *communed.* That is the most appropriate word I can think of to describe the transmission of verbal expressions, not in the form of sound waves as on Earth, but by direct transfer from mind to mind, a process in the course of which one has the illusion of hearing thoughts that another is having or at least desirous of expressing. It is for this reason that I'll use the words "commune" and "communed" to refer to thoughts exchanged face-to-face in heaven, though much of the time I'll simply use "say," "asked," "replied," and so forth, which, though not literarily accurate, serve well enough as metaphors.

I felt a jolt as this heavenly being communed to me:

Know this, Jack Treadwell: You stand before the designated greeter, the deputized judge, the welcomer or the reviler, Saint Peter if you fancy that myth, or even if you don't. Skip the Saint. Pete will do, or Sir, or Hey You, for I am any of these as you please. It matters not what you call me, only that I am the expression of God formed and fashioned within the limits of your comprehension.

There was nothing about this apparition that resembled my notion of Saint Peter, though the voice I heard, as I said, without agency of my ears but clearly in my mind, was deep, sonorous, and authoritative, as I imagined a saint in heaven should produce.

It may seem strange to you, but it did not occur to me that I might have been hallucinating or dreaming and that what I appeared to have witnessed was seemingly impossible. I don't know whether what follows is scientifically correct, but I have the impression that there is a faculty of the brain that detects impossibility or illogicality, and that when one is dreaming it is turned off. That was certainly true in this instance: the absurdity of St. Peter's referring to himself as the greeter, saying, for example, "Pete will do"—the phenomenal weirdness of the situation—failed to register.

My acceptance of what seemed the everyday ordinariness of the absurd continued. All the while, a central question kept running through my mind: Is this really St. Peter? If so, is he about to admit me to heaven, or will he cast me into hell? Other thoughts began forming but didn't reach the level of intelligibility before the shape, or figure, communed again:

What say you, Jack Treadwell?

"I . . . I don't know," I replied. "I can't believe I'm here. I need time to think."

Sheets of orange light, like heat lightning, flashed above, around, and below me, ratcheting up my anxiety.

I know your thoughts, Jack Treadwell. I know what happened every moment of your life.

I struggled not to be cowed, but I felt shocked and exposed. I thought of how important it is to be self-confident and assertive in life, and presumably thereafter. St. Peter had invited me to call him Pete, so I would! Hard upon that thought, I wondered whether this apparition in human shape who had said he was "the expression of God" was God himself, in diluted form perhaps, or only an individual shade like me, which would be the case if he was the shade of the original Peter, the rock on which Jesus said he would build his Church. (I'm not sure, but I think that's the "Peter" that tradition holds stands at the gates of heaven to judge the souls of the newly deceased.)

Another question I had was how God, or even Pete (St. Peter), could have time for a common shade like me. This stream of thoughts then reversed flow, and I reasoned that, since God can be everywhere, *is* everywhere, he could be with me if he wished or communing to me through St. Peter, yet be everywhere else at the same time. Of course that left standing the question: How could he do that?

I had never learned much about religion or theology, but I remembered reading that God shines with such glory that the sight of him would overwhelm anyone who looked at him. This was true of some of the Greek gods too, such as Demeter, who turned some poor fellow who saw her bathing in the nude into a stag, which was hunted down by his own dogs.

Another line of thought is that it would be impossible to look at God, because he is of a nature beyond human comprehension. The notion of an anthropomorphized God is a myth to modern theologians. I think I am right about that. If so, just as God does not present himself as something directly perceivable on Earth, neither does he in heaven!

It followed—I thought it followed at the time—that the shape who communed to me couldn't (or wouldn't) be God, but was merely the shade of a formerly living person. So the question became: Was this really St. Peter, or was it only an ordinary shade masquerading as him? It seemed to me that any such impostor would have been shipped off to hell long ago. So, I decided, bizarre as it might be, that the shape (the being) communing to me apparently was St. Peter or, more precisely, the shade of St. Peter himself.

Without planning to, I took a bold tack. "Look, Saint Peter," I communed. "I was a decent person. Sure I had plenty of failings, but if things are set up here to commit much of the human population to hell, to eternal torture, that would mean—and of course I hope this isn't true, surely it can't be—that God, and you who serve him, are, well, frankly, I would have to say, sadistic!"

Challenging God or even St. Peter could hardly have been a wise way to proceed. This seems obvious to me now, and I realize I might have seriously prejudiced my case, but please remember what pressure I was under—I was confused and frightened, hardly more capable of acting rationally than if I'd been in a dream.

By the way, I have a pretty good idea as to the psychological underpinning of my aggressiveness. I had decided while still in middle age that I had been too passive in life and had resolved to correct this tendency, among other ways by reminding myself not to be overly inhibited from asking questions or putting forth ideas. Through long experience I had learned, so I thought, that one should be assertive. Shun passivity. Be active, even aggressive, is the rule. Looking back, I think I failed to see that making such resolutions may be helpful, but actual situations tend to be nuanced. It's stupid to slavishly follow a general rule like "Be assertive." Yet that's what I was doing.

As it was, St. Peter didn't seem offended by my brash comment, and I felt free to continue:

"Pete" (I had decided to settle on this form of address), "May I ask a few questions?"

A few.

"The first is this: I was only one of billions of people on Earth. How could you know everything about me?"

The shape, Pete, communed again, this time in what seemed to me to be a critical tone.

For God and through God all things are possible.

"Yes, I realize that's true," I communed. "I should have thought of that. By the way, I was basically more like an agonistic than an atheist, if that matters. I wasn't like those people who disparage religion. I never meant any disrespect. I tried to be honest."

You were an atheist.

"Pete, Saint Peter, I cannot deny it. I just couldn't have faith."

You made no effort.

"True. You are right. I am truly very sorry."

As you can see, good-spirited readers, my show of assertiveness and self-confidence quickly gave way to fawning solicitude. Even at the time, I realized that my behavior was pathetic. Sniveling is no more effective in heaven than it is on Earth.

After I had uttered this apology for my atheism, Pascal's wager, or what I vaguely remembered was Pascal's wager, came to mind. He said something like, "The stakes are so high—an eternity in heaven or in hell—that one shouldn't risk not believing in God. You'd better be a believer!" I had never taken this theory seriously. Now, how I wished—

Pete's thoughts interrupted my own:

A poet wrote: "Oh God! If I worship thee in fear of Hell, burn me in Hell; and if I worship thee in hope of Paradise, exclude me from Paradise."

That was unexpected! It made me wonder whether this was still Pete or whether it might be God communing directly. Whoever it was, he knew I'd been thinking about Pascal's wager. He was rebuking me after reading my mind. Is this not the ultimate dystopia, where Big Brother not only controls your life but knows your every thought? I had been assuming I was in heaven, but this was more like hell. For all I knew, it was.

Pete again:

What say you now, Jack Treadwell?

He had said that I could call him Pete, and I had done so, but I now decided I should have been more respectful; I think I was afraid I would sound phony. I didn't want to be sycophantic like I'm sure many shades are. I was afraid Pete would see through any affectation; he might even see through a calculated attempt to be straightforward! It was a very uncomfortable situation.

2

I feel calm now writing about my initiation to the afterlife, but at the time I came close to screaming with frustration. I had to struggle to maintain any degree of equanimity. I was frightened.

At least I was aware of that and tried to have courage. I even ran through my mind, as I sometimes did during my most beleaguered moments when I was alive, Churchill's exhortation, "We shall fight on the beaches, we shall fight on the landing grounds, we shall fight in the fields and in the streets, we shall fight in—"

I caught myself before I finished, sensing that if God or Pete were listening—monitoring my mind—I would sound foolish to them, pathetic even. I was fleeing from reality, resorting to magical thinking. I had to do better. I must communicate forcefully and sincerely and avoid offensive accusations like implying that God and Pete might be sadistic, though that was the way I was beginning to think about them—but I must also avoid sounding abject. With this in mind I said:

"Excuse me, Pete, if this is you, or if you are God listening or speaking through Pete (Saint Peter), I am truly sorry. The stress must have gotten to me. I had thought that you, God, knew everything that will happen as well as everything that has happened and everything that is happening now, so you must know as well as I, or better than I, that what I would do or say is all pre-determined."

Pete had probably heard this before. In any case, he communed:

If God knew what was going to happen, he couldn't change it.

This sent a shudder through my body, or rather, since I had no body, through the form of the shade I had become. I knew I had to keep my wits, or more precisely, regain them, but before I could think what to say next, the voice that had been speaking in my mind yet again demanded:

What say you, Jack Treadwell?

Instead of answering immediately, I thought—this is awful. Why can't heaven be the way it's supposed to be?

Aware of what I was thinking, though I hadn't meant to communicate it to him, Pete interjected:

If it were, you'd already be in hell.

Pete's words (I had settled on being sure it was he), as I have said not spoken but perceived in my mind, had a weightier timbre than before, raising my anxiety to an even higher pitch and producing in me a sense of deepest unease. What I had experienced since I died contravened everything I knew. Yet what was happening was real. It was the real deal, *ha ha*. Why a silly joke and inappropriate thoughts that I couldn't suppress, though I knew they were probably flowing involuntarily from my mind to Pete's? I couldn't help myself, couldn't help my thoughts. Why did he keep asking, "What say you now?" He knew everything anyway! It was a test, obviously. A test. How could I meet it? I resolved as follows: I must root out pre-conceptions! I must take the test. And he knows that I think I must take the test. But I must tell him directly:

"A test. I understand completely Pete. It's right that you should give me a test."

This conciliatory thought was met by silence.

Time may have passed and possibly a great deal of it, though I couldn't tell how much, before I felt I must speak again, make an effort to defend myself:

"Pete, I have been thinking about how unkind I was to some people in my life, and not always honest, and sometimes hypocritical. I regret it so much."

The moment I said that, it occurred to me that I must sound like any one of countless other shades trying to ingratiate themselves with St. Peter. How paltry an offering. How phony. How often Pete must have heard it. How much he must despise it.

"I repent," I said gravely.

You rely on a myth. If it were of value for people to repent, everyone would constantly repent. There would be no incentive to be honest and kind. Feel regret, Jack. Feel remorse, but repent not.

I struggled to think what differences there were in these words. Should I tell Pete I felt remorse? I really did, as a matter of fact! Yes I should, I decided, but as sometimes happened to me when I was alive, though I planned to say one thing I said another:

"I'm sorry, Pete. I apologize. I thought repentance was important in Christianity."

Who said anything about Christianity?

Oh God, I thought, more confused than ever. Maybe this is the Judaic God, without Christ, or maybe it's even Allah, or who knows what other; maybe Hindu. Shiva is it? There was no way of telling. I would just have to assume it was the basic God, called different names by different faiths.

"Sorry," I said. "Forgive me, Saint Peter. Christianity happened to be the faith I was brought up in—"

That, of course, is why I appear to you as Saint Peter.

"Oh . . . I'm so sorry, Pete, Saint Peter. I should not have assumed, but I thought that to repent was a good thing in all religions, that, no matter what faith, God, that is, and you, Pete—looks, look favorably on—"

Carry a slate and wipe it clean whenever you want?

How could I answer that? Pete (or God) had driven me to despair. Despair in heaven! What irony. How unfair. How unjust. Good God, God and Pete are surely listening to my thoughts.

As a reeled-in fish flops helplessly in the net, ever weakening yet persisting in a life-death struggle to escape, I flopped. I must keep struggling. I must never give in. My destiny depended upon it!

On Earth in such circumstances I would have taken a deep breath. In heaven there was no need for it, or physical possibility, and so no restorative moment that might come with it.

"Even so, Saint Peter," I pleaded, "I hope you will find that I had a good heart and was generally a decent person and often kind or thoughtful toward others, and you will have mercy on me."

This latest formulation of contrition was met with a silence of unbearable weight and duration, in the course of which I felt myself shrinking into nothingness, certain that my divine fate had been decreed and would soon be executed.

READING THE LINES written above, I can see that I was functioning no better than an automaton programmed to say what would most likely elicit sympathy, giving no thought to searching my heart for what would be true and authentic and meaningful. *Heart?* An inept metaphor for a time when I had no physical body, no heart, nothing left of my earthly faculties other than a capacity to suffer.

I waited, endlessly it seemed, for Pete to respond. Churchill's "never surrender" coursed through my mind. Then, flailing about, trying to think of something acceptable: "Praise the Lord."

Pete instantly communed:

Praise the Lord? Do you think God is so petty that he wants humans to praise him?

"Oh, I'm sorry, Pete. I really am. I thought that to praise God is to show respect. Religious people on Earth praise God. They think it is pleasing to him."

He grew sick of it the first time he heard it.

"I'm so regretful. Believe me, I didn't know. I think that by saying 'Praise the Lord,' I meant well in thinking this. Believe me, how much I respect God."

God doesn't need your respect. It is you who need his respect!

"Oh, I understand. I'm so sorry. I should have realized."

Reduced to shards and splinters of my former self, I dug deep to find inner strength, deeper than ever when I was alive. Amazingly, like a gift from heaven, a bracing thought surfaced, a memory of a family conversation when I was a child. We were gathered for Sunday breakfast—Dad, Mom, my sister Karen, my other sister, Katie, and I. I don't remember what we were talking about or what set my dad off, but I remember him saying, "We Treadwells are made of sterner stuff." What a thrill I felt at the time. With this, what in retrospect strikes me as a pitiable stimulant, to fortify me, I imagined that I could convince Pete that I was worthy of salvation.

"Permit me to ask," I communed, "the belief people have that God is merciful—that is not a myth, is it?"

God is just.

"Just. Of course. I wouldn't want to say anything against justice, but I hope God thinks that being merciful is at least as important. As a great poet on Earth said, "The quality of mercy is not strained.""

Even as these thoughts streamed from my mind to Pete's, I was aware that I was making little sense, exposing my weak and meritless character and establishing ever more firmly that I was a worthless sinner, a sinner and a fool, digging a grave for myself as eternal and as deep as hell.

FOLLOWING THE EVENTS described above, Pete didn't communicate anything to me for what seemed an endless amount of time, and it may have been, because in heaven one has no sense of time, and time has no sense. But at some time (using the term metaphorically) it occurred to me that he shouldn't need *any* time to consider my case. Then, driven so close to the edge of madness that my thought processes spun into the farcical, the words ran though my mind: Surly, God, I mean not surly God, but *surely*. God could surely and not surly be . . . *ha ha*.

It took some effort, but I snapped out of this juvenile prattle, realizing that God himself was probably taking it in, knowing that he could think as fast as, probably faster than, lightning bolts travel that he hurls about the sky.

Failing in my efforts to be calm or take refuge in humor,

failing to retain any sense of perspective, failing to think of any persuasive or even intelligible argument as to why I should be saved; indeed, as is obvious now, teetering on the brink of insanity, I remembered: Of those things we cannot speak, we must remain silent. Wittgenstein. I think he said that it is for that reason it's useless to try to think what a lion would say. And Professor Nagel wrote about how you can't know what it's like to be a bat. What I'm driving at is that God and we are different species. Only from God's perspective it's humans and their shades who are lions and bats. Or maybe it's from a human's perspective that God is a lion or a bat. At least I had that much awareness—I mean that man and God exist on separate planes of existence and consciousness!

Courage, I told myself. And peace. Then, standing on what was no more substantial than a cloud in Earth's atmosphere, I tried to look respectful but not fearful, tried to seem self-assured about my worthiness, just as when facing a bear or other predator you mustn't let them sense your fear, not communicate that you are prey! Facing extinction, the prey prayed, *ha ha*.

As you can see, despite having resolved not to, once again I had spiraled into fatuity, despairing of thinking how to keep God from seeing my devious, petty, miserable, sniveling, self-serving self for what it was. Looking back, I can truly say that if insanity is a region of hell, I was there.

FOR A LONG time, as if there were time in heaven, no thoughts emanated from the shape before me that I'd come to know as Pete. Then he started moving on his cloudlet. I took insubstantial steps, then faster ones, trying to keep up, wondering if during the preceding lacuna he might have been consulting God.

"Pete," I called. "Pete!"

Yes.

"Has God said anything to you about . . . my future?"

Yes.

"What?"

About which circle you might be assigned to.

"Circle?

That's what I said.

"You don't mean of hell?"

What else?

"No, not hell! No! Please! Please!" I kept thinking the words: Not hell. Not an eternity of suffering. This couldn't be. Pete must be wrong. God wouldn't do this. He would have seen that I was trying to be whatever he wants, whatever it is. God loves me, shouldn't he? If only repenting meant something! Why had all the theologians and preachers misled us? I truly felt myself repenting, or was it only the *feeling* of repenting? Or the *felling* of repenting! *ha*. Felling on the way to falling on the way to being fallen. Man is fallen. Adam, not me. But Adam at least was not Cain!

I tried to rid myself of these inanities as fast as they sped through my mind: Retract them! Redact them! Wishful thinking. Wishful thinking was my way of being. So it went. I couldn't stop random thoughts from springing forth and careening into each other. Would this ever end? My mind was captive as if in a dream. In a dream you go with the dream. There is no free will in a dream. I had none now.

WE HAD REACHED the edge of a region of shades perched on closely packed cloudlets that I somehow perceived were near the edge of a precipice, and I saw other cloudlets, and shades walking off them, and cloudlets that were dissolving under others, shades falling one by one into the void, sometimes two by two, or two by three, or three by four, or more, all deep toward bottomless nothingness beneath us.

"Pete, don't let me fall!" I wailed. "Don't!"

Every pretense gone, every bit of sang-froid gone, I stood shaking, stripped of dignity, shamed in my despair, sustained by an insubstantial cloudlet that would support me only so long as God willed, feeling like an indiscernible flake of coal lodged in the depths of a cartload of coal in an endless procession of cartloads of coal, careening, riding, sliding one after another after another after another into the inexhaustible flames of hell.

3

Pete, communing to me again, this time with what registered as a snarky laugh:

Don't let me fall! They all say it.

If that was to make me feel frightened, it didn't work. To be honest, it did. But then I remembered that we Treadwells are made of sterner stuff. I yanked myself upright. Pete had talked about the circle of hell I *might* be assigned to. My cloudlet hadn't dissolved. I hadn't been judged. I still had a chance. In the distance I saw other shades on their cloudlets and took heart that they weren't drifting toward the invisible precipice I had perceived.

"Pete, just a minute," I communed, "if this is heaven, those shades have made it. They aren't going to hell, are they! If you get up to the edge and don't fall—and I didn't—you've made it. You're admitted to heaven. Right?"

What makes you think hell exists? The shades you saw falling are enjoying themselves. They land on a lower cloud and then float up again. It's part of the joy of being here.

I felt no relief hearing this. There was something ironic in Pete's tone. And he hadn't answered my question. Why would it feel good to plunge off a cloudlet not knowing where you might land? Was it supposed to be like riding a roller coaster?

Besides, I didn't see any shades rising; only falling. Pete was taunting me. Those shades who had fallen had probably been damned, and I might still be. Probably would be. Why was Pete so mean to me? I was in heaven, at least I thought so. Why wasn't I feeling eternal bliss? Why did I feel so bad about not having been a better person? All my angst should be behind me; yet regrets about my behavior, all the remorse I felt, weighed on me more heavily than ever.

I pulled myself together enough to ask a question that had been on my mind:

"Pete, you know, of course, of my wife, Ellie. She died a little over a year ago. She was a lovely person. I'm sure she must be here. Is there a way I can find her?"

Ellie is here; but really, Jack, you don't think you deserve the pleasure of seeing her, do you?

I shook off how that hurt and tried to think of the right words to say, but was no more capable of doing so than a clump of dirt. Finally, I couldn't restrain myself. "Stop playing cat and mouse with me, Pete! What's going to happen? Is God watching us? If you are, God, please forgive my sins and let me stay."

God isn't here.

"I thought God was everywhere, all the time."

He's coming back.

"What do you mean, 'coming back'?"

It is God's will that I should tend to you for a while.

"Tend to me? I can't see that you've tended to me so far. Taunted me is more like it. Why are you treating me this way?"

As you can see, my (I hope) sympathetic readers, what was happening was as bizarre as in a dream. But just as a skein of events unfolds in a dream and you don't consider whether they make sense—you don't say, "this is ridiculous, so it must be a dream"—I continued to be sure I could not be dreaming. I didn't see how I could be, because every sound and sight was clear and vivid, and there were no gaps in the succession of events.

Pete, as always, reading my thoughts:

You are right. This is no dream. God is everywhere and he is nowhere, which is to say you can't find him in a particular place. You can't determine even that he is a he. His nature surpasseth all understanding You asked about his "coming back." Coming back" is a figure of speech about the form he will assume to give you a feeling he's not talking on the speaker phone.

Speaker phone! God, it unnerved me the way Pete switched from the kind of talk you'd expect in the Bible and everyday talk on Earth. I looked over the edge of my cloudlet and thought of plunging into the void—get it over with—then realized you can't end your life when you're not alive.

"Pete, I may only have been in heaven a few minutes or hours, if I'm guessing right about how much time has passed on Earth since I died, but I spent a long time being alive, and I can tell when someone's not being straight with me."

What happened next knocked my socks off, as living people are wont to say. Pete's tone changed completely. I must have said something that jolted him out of the role he was playing, which thus far had been that of a prosecutor bullying the defendant, for now, to my surprise, he communed:

Your frustration is understandable. I have not been myself with you. I have not been expressing God's will. In one holy sense, I shouldn't tell you this, but in another holy sense I should. This has been an extraordinarily unusual what you'd call a day here. There has never been a what you'd call a day here like it.

"Huh? What's different?"

We have a strange situation developing in heaven, and it has affected my ability to commune with you.

"I believe you, Pete. Please tell me about it."

What is happening now has never happened before, at least not in the two Earth millennia I have been here.

"What? Tell me!"

God has fallen ill.

"Pete, I believe you wouldn't lie to me, so I have to assume that you sometimes kid around. I know God has emotions, like feeling infinite love for everyone and getting angry and occasionally wrathful, but this is *God* we're talking about. There is no way he could fall ill."

Out of nothingness Pete produced a halo and like some expert Frisbee player tossed it so it hovered just above my head. And, as in some depiction of Christ in a medieval painting, it stayed there. I was impressed.

You can't keep it. It's just temporary, like a lei they hang on tourists' necks when they arrive in Hawaii.

Which *is* permanent, I thought, except the flowers fade, but a halo shouldn't. I thanked Pete even so, and hearing a note of gratitude in my voice, I remembered something about intermittent reinforcement being the strongest form of conditioning. Could this be Pete's way of softening me up, keeping me off guard, inducing me to fall prey to the "Stockholm syndrome," in which people held hostage develop a perverse feeling of camaraderie with their captors? The notion of God not feeling well was beyond belief. How could such a thing happen? Where would it lead?

Stop whining, Treadwell, I told myself. What Pete is saying could provide an opening. Think pragmatically. You're fighting for your life, or rather your death, your future in eternity!

"What could have made God ill?" I asked. "He has unlimited power; he owns the whole universe; he could *will* himself to be well."

He could, but he can't, because he's depressed. And not all the power in the universe can change it, because it reflects his true feeling.

I couldn't understand how this could be so. It wasn't possible.

Pete, receiving my thoughts, communed:

It has to be possible, because it's happened! Pay heed, Jack. The realm in which you lived is material. God is not concerned with material things. He is spiritual through and through, and this is a spiritual matter.

"Not concerned with what he created? Not concerned about the seven billion people on Earth? That's not what religious people think!"

God's thinking is not affected by what religious people think.

"Why did he become depressed?"

God allowed humans freedom even though it might produce evil, which it did. He's begun to think that it was a bad idea.

"But *not* giving them freedom would have been a bad idea!"

Precisely so, and dwelling on that is depressing.

"It took him all this time to feel this way?"

I never got an answer to this question, for the apparition I had known as Pete dissolved in front of my eyes, as did the halo over my head, leaving me alone, strangely thinking of Wordsworth's poem about wandering as lonely as a cloud, then thinking of a sign I had seen in front of the church down the road from Arcadia Retirement Estates: IF YOU FEEL GOD ISN'T CLOSE, GUESS WHO MOVED.

Well, there was no doubt that this time it was God, or at least Pete, who had moved! A fair-weather friend, I thought, absurdly, and began to feel sorry for myself. Then I thought how blasphemous I must sound. Depressed or not, God was probably listening to my thoughts. Unless he has the kind of sense of humor I've seen no evidence of, I'm finished, through, *finis, finito*, sadly gone and done for. I indulged myself with such nonsense until I had sunk into a maudlin stupor, a state of depression possibly deeper even than God's.

Here is some advice for you, my good and noble readers: Never despair! Like the sun bursting forth after a summer storm, Pete returned with this hopeful news:

God has not abandoned you, Jack. It is impossible that he would abandon anyone. But on this what on Earth you would call a day he is gravely out of sorts. He is telling me to do things he never has before and not telling me to do things he always has before. I was about to judge you, but I am not able to do so. For the first time since I ascended here, I am not able to discern God's will. When I cannot discern God's will, I cannot discern my own will. The truth is, Jack: Heaven has fallen into disarray.

As I absorbed this, I saw an opportunity. "Pete," I asked, "could you admit me to heaven on your own initiative? Special circumstances? You've been on this job almost two millennia, right? You should have a pretty good idea of what God's will would be even if he hasn't told you, right?"

You want to be admitted to heaven?

"Well, of course!"

You shouldn't be so sure you'll like it.

"What do you mean?"

Since I have no shades to judge until God is able to express his will, I'll take you on a tour; it may change your mind.

"A tour of heaven?"

A small region of it.

"I'd like that," I said. "But this makes me wonder all the

more about something that's been bothering me. I don't understand how you can spend so much time with me. I mean hundreds of thousands of people must arrive here every day. Yet, you seem to have all the time in the world. I guess I mean all the time *out* of the world. Can you talk to every new shade at once? Can God be listening to everyone—shades and living people—at the same time? How can this happen? If you think about it, maybe you can appreciate why I'm an atheist. I mean *was* an atheist. Is God like some kind of cosmic computer that can—"

Sensing that Pete was getting impatient, I stopped thinking in mid-sentence. My mind went limp. Pete communed:

What you are thinking of is a primitive analogy of God's powers. God can hold all information in the universe in his mind and continuously update it. And to some extent even I can. Processing data instantaneously removes time as a factor. If there are hundreds of thousands of shades from planet Earth alone to be judged each what you call a day, it's as if there are hundreds of thousands of iterations of me to judge them. But this only hints at God's power, which is as far advanced of any human conception of what can be achieved by a quantum computer as a quantum computer is over an archaic human counting on his fingers.

Another lacuna ensued, perhaps because I was overtaxed by Pete's explanation of how divine beings function. Time may have passed without anything happening, or, I suppose, things may have happened without time passing. In any event, I was becoming increasingly uneasy because Pete had said he would give me a tour, but it had never begun.

I tried to achieve a measure of composure. Pete was obviously confused by God's behavior or condition. He seemed to be trying to act responsibly, and he seemed to have become more favorably disposed toward me. Still, the way he had taunted and badgered me was disturbing. In these circumstances I could think of nothing to do but to wait patiently and be careful not to irritate him.

That's what I did, and it was apparently a sound policy. After what on Earth I would think was an extraordinary additional lapse of time, he motioned for me to follow him. We moved slowly at first, then faster, floating through clusters of cloudlets scattered at such distances that I could discern shades perched on only the nearest of them. Pete explained that personal cloudlets weren't really needed—God created them to give shades the familiar feeling of something like earth under their feet.

He continued on at an even faster pace. Like a dog following his master, ignorant of his destination but obliged to trust him, I trailed along in his wake.

4

Why was Pete in such a hurry? On Earth I might have thought he wanted to save time. Since in heaven there is no time to be saved, I concluded he must be distraught. I had difficulty keeping up with him, which of course was entirely psychological, for it's in the nature of heaven that, generally, no effort is involved in movement at whatever speed you like.

I had no idea how far we would have to travel, but it didn't seem to matter: I felt neither hunger, thirst, nor feeling of fatigue. Have I mentioned that in heaven bodily processes are absent, presumably because they would be inappropriate in God's spiritual realm? It was for this reason that I knew I could trail along behind Pete for hours, indeed years, millennia, even eons. That was an insight into heaven's strange workings or non-workings, and it worried me: Conceivably I had entered into a paradise that would become a hell of boredom. I began thinking of Dante's *Divine Comedy*, which I had read in translation when I was in my twenties, almost sixty years before I died, remembering little, of course, except that *Il Inferno* was the most interesting and lively place, *Il Purgatorio* less so, and *Il Paradiso* positively stifling—all those saints and other good and pious folk arrayed in the firmament like ornaments on a Christmas tree. Beatrice, who sent Dante into raptures of ecstasy when they were kids, had lost not a smidgeon of her earthly beauty in heaven, but she struck me as somewhere between dull and duller. How did she stand it? Why wasn't it a real downer for Dante, to see her propped there like a bauble on a shelf? Could she really get that much out of contemplating the glory of God day after day, a thousand ages after a thousand ages?

Ahead of us lay more cloudlets. I could see through some of them as if I had X-ray vision. I could even see through the shades perched on them. They didn't obscure my sight of the expanses beyond, which seemed to extend infinitely in all directions.

A cloud with an elderly female figure on it glided into view, a shade like me. All of us, I was to learn, shared certain characteristics in our afterlife, being incorporeal, of varying ages but with few exceptions relatively trim and lithe, phantasmal in appearance, yet, through some divine process the nature of which I could never imagine much less understand, clearly recognizable as the living persons we once were, and garbed most commonly among all types and both sexes as one might expect of ballet performers or participants in a gymnastics competition.

This first shade I encountered had a kindly expression. Just from looking at her I could tell that she must have been selfless and compassionate while alive. It made me feel like a crumb. She was the kind of person who deserved to be here, whereas I was probably here only because God was depressed and the process of judging had been held up.

This beneficent old shade extended simulacra of her hands. I held out the simulacrum of my right hand and she embraced it as if within her palms. The truth hit me: This shade of a good woman saw directly into my soul. All the guilt I had suppressed for treating people badly during my life leaped to the surface of my consciousness with such force that I had the feeling I might be in hell rather than in heaven, and that part of my punishment was to confront each instance of my bad behavior and see it for what it was instead of forgetting about it or trying to justify it.

"It's all right, friend," this kindly shade communed. "You are here now. God loves you. When fortune smiles on you, be accepting of it."

"Thank you," I said. "But I can't help feeling guilty. I hurt people."

"We all did," she said, and made a gesture that suggested to me that if we had been alive and on Earth she would have caressed my cheek. "God forgives you. Those whom you hurt forgive you. That is God's way."

I wasn't at all sure it was God's way, and I doubted even more that it was the way of some people I'd hurt. Still, I felt better after this encounter. It raised my hopes that I might attain permanent residency.

Pete, looking on, communed the equivalent of a smile, though one that, as I thought about it, was more of a smirk. Then the kindly shade was gone. I sensed I wasn't forgiven after all, but I couldn't dwell on that further. Pete was floating along and picking up speed. I hurried effortlessly to keep up with him.

Ahead of us were steep banks of clouds with tremendous vertical drops. Celestial lights, pink and bluebird blue, flashed forth from them, and I saw scores, hundreds, of shades gliding down and through clouds, then ascending like flocks of eagles lifted on thermals, then diving as if to seize prey. Pete explained:

These are shades who lived good lives. They were kind to others and unkind to no one, and when they failed in any respect, they felt remorse and tried to do what they could to make up for it.

I considered how this compared with my own behavior. What a gap, a chasm. During my lifetime I had felt resentful toward people who had treated me badly but given no thought to how contemptible my own behavior had been. Now, in heaven of all places, self-loathing was pursuing me, threatening to overwhelm me, shaping my mood, enveloping my being. Maybe this would be my salvation, I imagined. Maybe this was the way heaven *is*.

After we had drifted past this region of shades who had lived good lives, time may have passed. How much was indeterminable, but I remember that I spent the whole of it dwelling on my lapses and transgressions, an exercise that caused what had merely been a disquieting speculation to segue first into a dark fear and then into a firm conviction that I had already been, or soon would be, irrevocably, hopelessly damned.

We approached a small cloud. It was higher than ours, but we rose smoothly to its level. Pete communed:

You're in luck.

Two figures were standing on it, and as we grew closer, I could see that they were engaged in conversation. Closer still, I blinked in astonishment at the two shades, photographs of whom when they were living beings were etched in my mind: one very tall and with a trim black beard and the other with a bushy gray one—Abraham Lincoln and Walt Whitman! If they are here, surely this is heaven, I thought, and heaven is where I am!

I wondered what they were talking about and whether they had been conversing since the great poet joined our fallen president here more than a hundred years ago. I wanted to ask Pete if we could float closer to their cloudlets, but he communed a negative answer with a shake of his incorporeal head.

On we floated, and I noticed many shades that were children, some only toddlers, and a mother holding her baby, so tiny—a newborn I thought—too young I would think to have been baptized, suggesting that the Roman Catholic business about such unfortunates being consigned to limbo was a complication invented by man and not by God.

Pete communed to me in as kindly a tone as I'd yet sensed: *You have some religious spirit, despite your atheism.*

"It's hard to remain an atheist when you're in heaven," I said.

Pete exuded the equivalent of a benevolent smile, but my mood was shifting again to the dark side. Whatever was occurring—and it was a long way from being clear what that was—was more unsettling than reassuring. I had returned to thinking that though God may be depressed and my fate delayed, my chances of being saved were nil.

I was distracted again as another figure passed by, one vaguely familiar, perhaps an inhabitant of the eighteenth century.

Pete communed:

Do you know who that is?

"No, but I almost do. Maybe it will come to me."

Bach.

"J. S. Bach?"

Himself.

"Fantastic."

Mozart is here too.

"But he was quite a sinner, wasn't he?"

More than Earth's historians realize; but God wrote his music for him and couldn't bear to turn him away.

"Really! Pete, could I hear Bach play the organ or harpsichord? Do they have any in heaven?" It seemed unlikely, but I was thinking that with God all things are possible.

Pete's incorporeal being seemed to mask a smile.

Yes, with God all things are possible. There is no limit to what he can do, but not for you.

This cutting remark raised my anxiety to its highest level yet. I glanced around, for some reason expecting a thunderbolt, then recalling that it was Zeus, a mere mythological character, who employed this means of terrorizing mortals. So far, in heaven, I'd only seen lightning, and that was more like summer heat lightning than those dazzling jagged flashes favored by wrathful gods. I smiled for a moment (a nervous smile, I'm sure), then thought: Shades of those who have lived good lives reach eternal bliss in heaven, but, do they ever smile? The answer, I can report, is that they do, in most cases like Mona Lisa.

Pete, humming, then singing:

He is trampling out the vintage where the grapes of wrath are stored / He hath loosed the fateful lightning of his terrible swift sword.

For some reason this brought to mind Kierkegaard's fear and trembling—I think it's actually fear and trembling and sickness unto death. For me: fear and trembling *after* death and plenty of it. Pete, continuing:

He is sifting out the hearts of men before his judgment seat.

On we floated. I had a dreamy sensation as if still on morphine drip in the hospice. Events occurred. I can't be sure how many I remember, but one in particular stayed with me: a pale-cheeked, rather rotund male figure waved at me from the cloudlet he bestrode, lifting my spirits. I waved back. Pete communed:

God, in his mysterious ways, is allowing you to see some famous shades. Whimsical of him, in my opinion, but it may be a sign he's feeling better. If so, I rejoice.

"This shade may be famous, Pete, but I don't recognize him."

The beneficent figure passing us waved again, finishing with the sign of the cross.

It's a pope! They are extremely rare here. That you are looking at one is through God's grace, not in accord with the laws of probabilities, I can assure you.

A pope, really? Which one?

John the Twenty-Third. Not the infamous John the Twenty-Third, circa *fourteen hundred, but Angelo Roncalli, the jolly pope, who occupied the Holy See briefly when you were a young man. You know—and I'm not necessarily talking about popes now, though I could be—there are hordes of people with esteemed reputations who were never allowed to stay here. They had dark secrets even close friends and family members were unaware of, but God knew everything about them, of course, and so they were hurled into hell. Most of them were surprised to find themselves there, because they had fooled themselves into thinking they were good people, just as they had fooled others.*

Pope John XXIII waved at me again, and I waved back, and for some reason the exchange made me feel better than I had since I'd arrived in heaven. Then I remembered what Pete had said about shades who were surprised to find themselves in hell.

"Didn't you tell me earlier that there isn't any hell?" I exclaimed.

Let me ask you a couple of things, Jack. One: Define what you think hell is.

"The worst possible condition a shade could be in?"

Excellent answer. Two: Which would be worse: going to hell if you had known that there was one, or going to hell if you had been certain there was no such thing?

"I suppose going to hell if you'd been certain there was no such thing."

Then, if God told you that hell existed, you'd be expecting it, which would mean that the hell you reached wouldn't be the worst possible condition, but because hell has to be the worst possible condition, God, and I through whom he acts, has to tell you that it doesn't exist.

I was stunned. How duplicitous. How diabolical. "Pete," I protested, "this is so different from standard Christian theology, and so different from how people imagine God to be like. So it's all the worse when you get there?"

Precisely.

"This seems so cruel."

Humans are cruel when they hurt each other despite having the choice not to. God has no choice. This is the holy order of things.

"I thought God was omnipotent, that he could make any choice he wanted, but for humans choices are constrained by our pasts, our environments. Things are pretty much predetermined, aren't they? To a large extent we have only the illusion of choice. So humans should get some compassion from God. If God is omnipotent, he ought to give people a break."

God is all wise and all loving. Those principles govern every choice he makes. Therefore he has no choice but to follow them.

What's all loving about sending ordinary people like me to hell?

God's love is just.

Well, my (I hope) faithful readers, you can see that whatever I might say, Pete would stick up for God, so I decided not to argue. I would just try to get information, hoping I could learn something that could help me.

Deciding that hell almost certainly existed despite Pete's confusing statements, I asked: "What percent of shades are sent to hell?"

I don't keep track, but I'd guess about ninety-five percent.

"Holy shiiii . . . Pete, that's surely excessive. It's terrible. Everybody has flaws, done things they wouldn't be proud of, but most people are well-meaning, decent most of the time, doing their best to be good citizens."

Like you think you were?

"Not think. I really was, Pete."

Ah, you're exhibiting pride! Sinning even in heaven!

But his anger, or scorn, or playful teasing, or whatever it was, instantly passed. He gestured to my right:

"Don't look now . . . I bet you recognize her!"

This time I knew the face at once. She was one of the most famous movie stars of all time—Ingrid Bergman! Looking as she did in her prime!

"I have to admit it's a pleasure to behold her," I said. "I didn't know she was a saint, or however near a saint you have to be to stay here."

Pete glanced around in all directions. For the first time it was he, rather than I, who seemed nervous and uncomfortable. He drew closer to me—I could sense the enormous power immanent in his quasi-divine presence.

I've never said this to anyone before, but I'll tell you something. She wasn't even close to being a saint. She got into heaven solely on her looks and talent.

You're kidding.

I never kid. God himself told me that he couldn't stand the thought that the Devil would be able to look at her for an eternity instead of him.

"But there must be millions of beautiful women who went to hell. The Devil must find consolation in that."

Consolation and frustration: The Devil can only look at them.

"You mean God can . . . more than looking—" I broke off in mid-thought, afraid of uttering a really bad blasphemy.

Pete was looking at the cloud beneath us. He didn't want to pursue the subject. He may even have been worried about what God might think of him for having brought it up, a thought that stirred in me an echo of the schadenfreude I so often felt when I was alive, sinfully I now realized.

I might have dwelled on this further had not a female figure appeared before us and alighted near my cloudlet. It was the shade of Sue Marcello, whom I knew, oh so long ago, and yet the time when we were together seemed as if yesterday, as if this very day. In fact she had never left my mind, though we had, oh so long ago, said good-bye, and she looked as I remembered her, stunning as she was then; and even though we were in heaven, there was nothing amorphous about her, because, I dimly realized, she was no mere shade, she was now an angel, and one, by her appearance, of high station in God's esteem; yet I had taken up with someone else, a stupid fling that quickly became stale until I fled it, but in my then base state wanted to grasp for any kind of acceptability no matter how insipid, inauthentic, and purposeless a life I might be embracing, thinking that nothing more would remain to me. Only through great good fortune, did I find . . . but I won't go on about that, for here was Sue with a smile, a smile I could read in all its complexity. She hadn't forgotten how mendacious I had been, what a loathsome rogue, what a knave and a fool; but angel that she was now and, sadly too late I realized, was *then*, I could sense how profoundly she understood me, understood that I had been morally and spiritually ill-formed, that I was to some degree a good person, that I could have been a lot better than I was, except I couldn't because I was in the grip of the forces that had shaped me. I had been damaged and was destined to damage others. I hoped she understood. Or was this wishful thinking? All of it wishful thinking. Oh, the folly of hope!

Sue floated off; yet her image, her persona, remained in my consciousness and became a reality that transcended the entire firmament stretched through space—the entire spacescape of clouds and delicate blue light and ascended souls, and beyond them, perhaps, black space and stars. Was Sue no less ravishing than Dante's Beatrice? I asked myself, at the same time wondering if this was a lascivious thought, a base emotion of the sort you must shed if you want to preserve a chance that the gates of heaven will open.

What folly my life had been, and even in heaven I felt ill-formed, retrogressing while trying to imagine I was attaining a more enlightened state.

Pete entered my consciousness again, gesturing with the simulacrum of his long sleeved arm:

You are thinking that you don't deserve to be here. You don't. God has his reasons, it is often said, though none that would favor you.

Knowing not how to respond to this, I let it drop. We floated on. My thoughts became gauzier. Pete communed several times, but I was insensible to his observations. I was still thinking of Sue Marcello, thinking how I should have gone to hell for the way I had treated her if for nothing else. Then, that perhaps most appalling of all speculations revisited my mind. Might what I had thought was heaven be only the first chapter of an eternity in hell, God's ironic way of flinging injustice in my face?

Another of those lacunae ensued, then Pete communed:

I've enjoyed this tour so much, I almost forgot about the crisis.

"Oh, the crisis in heaven. I hope it's resolved all right, and that God is feeling better," I said, and instantly regretted it because I didn't mean it. I only cared about myself not getting sent to hell and knew that Pete knew that I didn't give a fig's leaf for God or for him. It was another instance of digging a hole for myself, lowering myself a step closer to hell. Best to change the subject and hope he wouldn't think about it.

"My grandfather must be here," I communed. "He was a kindly old gentleman, though he died when I was only ten years old and I never learned much about him."

Your grandfather Thomas? He was one of those with the dark secrets I mentioned. Even their best friends and family members didn't learn about them.

"Really? What were his dark secrets? I'd be curious to know."

For what would have been a long time if time passed in heaven, Pete was silent. Finally, he communed:

You had six half aunts and half uncles you never knew about, four of whom he *never knew about.*

Pete's disclosure of sins of my grandfather cut to the center of my being. I had thought of Grandpa Tom as almost a saint and had entertained a notion that in goodness, faithfulness, honesty, and compassion I ranked only a few notches below him. I still felt a few notches below him, but he had slid down toward the bottom of the scale.

5

After dropping that bombshell about my grandfather, Pete dissolved from my sight, but before doing so, he communed that regardless of God's illness, the time was near at hand when I would be judged. In heaven, where any consideration of time is problematical, that could mean anything, but I knew I couldn't rest easy; I must keep working to improve my chances.

After one of those lacunae, which on Earth might be attributed to a period of unconsciousness, let's say sleep, but may simply have been one when events occurred I participated in but did not remember, I became aware that I was on my former cloudlet and Pete was again beside me. From the moment I'd arrived in heaven my moods had swung wildly. Now I was overcome with apprehension, convinced that the preliminaries were over and I was about to be judged.

Not at the moment, it turned out. Pete, whose moods seemed as volatile as mine (assuming that he wasn't acting, playing the role of chief intimidator), communed cheerily:

Welcome back. There are some people here you've heard of.

We were floating in the direction of the shade of a gentleman of middle years dressed rather quaintly, I thought, as if from a bygone age. He turned and addressed me:

"You arrived here recently?" He said this in English, though with a heavy French accent.

Pete, knowing I was wondering who had addressed me, communed that it was the esteemed essayist, Michel de Montaigne.

"Marvelous!" I communed.

I would have liked to have discussed some of Montaigne's famous essays with him, but I hadn't read any of them. One of them had been assigned in a college course I took, but I had only glanced at a classmate's notes on it.

"I am so honored to meet you," I tried to commune, but even as the words passed through my mind, Montaigne was gone. Doubtless he found me of little interest.

Pete, switching to didactic mode, communed:

I have admired Michel ever since he arrived here what would be four or five centuries ago in Earth time. Whenever I encounter him, I think, here is the shade of a man who embraced life, enlarged life, and fulfilled himself. That is the challenge for humans. They must be open to life. Not so were you, Jack. Early in your youth you spun a cocoon about yourself and spent your days squeezed into it. Now, in heaven, your shade is fluttering like a butterfly, soon to—

He broke off as another figure entered into our presence, the shade of a gentleman with a warm and inquiring expression in his eyes.

Jorge Luis Borges, Pete communed.

I gaped in astonishment. "Ah, the great Argentinian writer!"

This esteemed figure came closer, and I felt a sensation as if he were gripping my right hand, which of course he was not.

"Great Argentinian writer?" Does that phrase suggest to you that I might have read at least one of Borges's stories or essays? In truth I had not. My habit of shameless posturing had followed me to heaven. Too late I caught myself indulging in my earthly habit of trying to impress people at the cost of misleading them. Pete, of course, saw my affectation for what it was.

Borges drifted on. I had an even greater shock as I recognized the next famous personage. As far as I knew he wasn't even dead yet! Nor was he one who, in my opinion, had any right to be in heaven. Yet here he was, wearing a happy, self-satisfied smile on his incorporeal face. Unmistakably the figure before me was Newt Gingrich!

"I can't believe this," I said to Pete. "He was one of the most smug, snide, self-serving, snake oil salesmen in American politics, and there was plenty of competition. I didn't know he was dead. How did he get here?"

Calling someone names instead of stating facts? Is that one of your habits you think will allow you to stay in heaven?

"Oh, I'm so sorry, Pete. Forgive me. I will never do that again. Still, I must honestly say I'm surprised to see him here."

What you see is an illusion. Newt isn't here, but he so often dreams he is that God transformed one of his dreams into what on Earth might be a holographic video so all of us can see Newt's dream as well as he can. I know this seems strange to you, and it does to me too. As God's emotional illness was taking shape, he began developing little quirks of this sort— ways of amusing himself, I suppose. I think he was trying to fend off the deep depression he felt coming on. He must have hoped that having, not Newt, of course, but Newt's dream floating about heaven would lift his spirits.

"Goodness, God is even more mysterious in his ways than I had imagined."

Of course there is a darker interpretation to this. Allowing Newt to dream that he is in heaven may make it all the more hellish for him when he learns his ultimate fate. As I told you, hell is worse if you didn't think you were going to go there.

"You mean God is planning to send Newt to hell?"

Not necessarily. The same that may be said of him may be said of you. And the same that may be said of you may be said of him.

It wasn't clear what Pete was implying by this latest in a long line of cryptic statements, but if he meant that my fate was intertwined with Newt's, it wasn't a good sign. Once again I shuddered, my anxiety approaching what on Earth might be diagnosed as a psychotic state, one that was threatening to become my habitual way of being.

Pete's next thought coursed through my mind:

It's time.

"Time for what?"

To evaluate your life: To decide how you measured up.

You mean you're going to judge me.

God judges you through me. Let us begin.

"But don't you have to wait to learn God's will?"

It's not wise for you to try to thwart me.

"I'm not. But—"

Let us begin.

What did I do wrong? I was a decent man!

Let me count the ways: You settled for being mediocre, thought poorly of yourself, shrank back from achieving anything of significance. Yet you were in awe of successful people. Envy was your defining state of mind.

"These may have been failings of mine, but they weren't harmful to others. I shouldn't be condemned just for being ordinary. I was generally a kind and sensitive person."

Such was the perception you created and nurtured. But your

*weaknesses, your settling for the ordinary, your lack of courage, hurt
others. You mistreated Lisa.*

"No, it was Sue. Never Lisa."

Both.

"Really that's not so. Lisa was cold to me—"

I was silenced by the look Pete gave me; it carried the message that my memory of my relationship with Lisa was distorted at best.

What could I do in these circumstances? Pete had sometimes been helpful, almost friendly—he had confided to me about God's emotional state; he had taken me on a tour, but just as often, more often, he had taunted, badgered, and threatened me, and accused me of the basest things, and driven me to despair. It was maddening, and I had been made mad. No use hiding, no use defending myself, I decided. I must confess, not deny, especially since Pete can see into my mind, know my every thought. Oh, what a hateful thing is heaven. Sorry, God, I didn't mean that. I'm sorry if I offended thee.

"All right, it's true," I exclaimed. "In each case, I became interested in someone else, but—"

It was more complicated than that.

"What do you mean?"

You were afraid.

"Huh? What would I have had to be been afraid of?"

Exactly.

I made no response, for Pete was communing silently but unequivocally that, with every word I spoke, I was digging deeper the hole that would soon receive me into its depths.

*You were afraid of success, afraid of commitment. You were selfish.
You mistreated Laurie, Marianne, and Lily, even your mother. You*

were gratuitously and baselessly contemptuous of others, rarely went out of your way to help others, had false ideals, were generally oblivious to how anyone but you was feeling, and never inquired into your own failings. You were a reckless, feckless, lecherous, treacherous, kindless, villainous monster, albeit of a lesser sort.

"That hurts. But Marianne? I don't remember anyone named Marianne."

That's precisely why she's on the list.

Head bowed, I communed: "I do feel remorse, Pete. Even when I was alive, I felt remorse, and it was remorse over hurting others. When a person feels that way, isn't that where God's infinite mercy comes into play?"

But Pete was gone, and I had a headache, though I had no head in the physical sense. My mind is a blank about what happened next. I only know that it seemed like I was sleeping and then that I was waking up in the hospice, sort of waking up, because I was feeling drugged and in some kind of stupor. Opening my eyes, I saw a nurse and Dr. Kapp standing by my bed.

"This is a miracle," said the nurse.

"Not a miracle," said Dr. Kapp. "But close to it. An extraordinary remission."

A glaring white light hurt my eyes. I shut them tight as I could.

Someone else entered, a woman, I guessed, by the sound of sharp heels on the floor.

"Still alive?" someone said.

"We're thrilled," said Dr. Kapp.

The glare of the light hurt my eyes, though they were shut tight. Others were entering.

"Still here?" a new voice said. "You'll have to move him to

the hospital or elsewhere. He's exceeded the maximum stay allowed. Doctor, you said he'd be dead within four days; it's already been nine."

"It might kill him to move him now," said Dr. Kapp.

"Sorry. That's the rule."

"You can't do this," someone cried. I recognized her voice; she'd been my nurse earlier.

"Oh yes we can," the other voice retorted. "We set the rules here, and you agreed to abide by them when we gave you privileges."

"But a life is at stake," said Dr. Kapp.

"Maybe so, but you knew that it might be when you agreed to our terms as a condition of admitting him."

"What's the insurance situation?" my nurse asked. "Maybe it's covered."

"Doesn't matter. We made commitments to other doctors and patients to make the space available."

The voices of the participants in this colloquy had been rising. There was the sound of scuffling; I felt a rip of pain in my arm as a tube pulled out. The noise was unbearable, just as the light had been. I had been able to close my eyes, but I couldn't close my ears. I screamed, and the sound of my scream was the worst pain of all.

Then I felt relaxed. Apparently I was awake again. For a few moments it seemed that I was back in heaven; then that I was nowhere, impossible as that would be; then back in heaven. Yes, that was it. I was floating on my cloudlet. What a relief to have escaped from Earth! Not really from Earth, of course, but from a dream of being on Earth, a nightmare! Who would think such an experience possible in heaven?

Though I was glad that this distasteful episode was over, a

deep sense of melancholy enveloped me. For a few moments, horrible as the dream had been, my life had been restored during it, only to be taken away again, and I remembered all the more intensely the wonder of being alive.

6

In heaven, as on Earth, you have to keep reevaluating your situation and your goals. Of course, as an atheist, I had not believed in heaven, but once I'd arrived and was seemingly indisputably standing before St. Peter, I had to revise my thinking. When I was an Earthling, I thought as an Earthling, but when I became a shade in heaven, I put away Earthly thoughts. At least I tried to.

When I met Pete, I assumed that he would either admit me to heaven or send me to hell, where I presumably belonged. Instead, he had been equivocal and cryptic. His swings of mood were not, one would think, a fitting characteristic for a saint. To be fair, God's illness had precipitated what was surely the most stressful period in Pete's two thousand years on the job, and I was hardly in a position to complain at having arrived when heaven was wrenched by chaos. Had it not been for that, flames might by now be licking up my legs.

In my isolation I could think coolly about my situation, but I still had no idea what to make of it. For a while, I had hoped to be admitted as a permanent resident. But then Pete had laid it out to me: I didn't deserve to be in heaven, and not just because I had been an atheist. That wasn't the end of it. Conditions in heaven weren't what anyone on Earth would have imagined. Who would have thought that yes, God exists, but he can become emotionally unstable?

God's illness may have had the effect of my getting a temporary reprieve, but it would have been foolish to imagine that he wouldn't recover and give Pete the go-ahead to judge me. In fact, there was a good chance that he had already done so and that Pete was simply turning the screws tighter before sending me to hell.

He had made it clear that God had "little quirks," like displaying Newt Gingrich's dream as if it were a YouTube diversion for the amusement of everyone in heaven. Another quirk seemed to be a penchant for confounding and terrorizing hapless shades like me.

It was at this juncture in my ruminations that a bold idea came to mind. I would escape. Not to Earth of course—there could be no chance of that since it would require coming back to life—but to a safe place in heaven, out of Pete's sight, and even out of God's sight maybe, though of course not out of range of his peripheral vision. God and Pete had plenty to think about besides me. People were dying all over the world, their shades congregating at the gates of heaven like clouds of newly hatched gnats over a stagnant pond. The backlog must be growing by the minute.

God and Pete seemed capable of doing everything at once, but this unprecedented jam-up of applicants (perhaps better designated supplicants) might open up options for imaginative shades like me. If I was bold and resourceful enough, I might succeed in escaping scrutiny. How delicious it would be not only to attain permanent residency in heaven, but to have tricked my way into it!

I wondered if any other shades had thought of escaping

judgment. Damn few, I guessed. The tendency when you get to heaven is to think that you have to obey orders and be docile. How could you possibly outwit God? But that might be just why I could get away with it. They (God and Pete) would never expect me to try such a thing. Then I thought of Satan, and how he thought he could get away with rebelling. He was sent to hell and, although some people and, as I understand it, even theological scholars, at least of the fundamentalist persuasion, think Satan has a rousing good time making mischief on Earth, the fact is that he *was* consigned to hell, and it can't be very pleasant there.

Satan challenged God directly, which in my judgment was a big mistake. My strategy would be quite the opposite: to get as far away as I could on my cloudlet and keep outside of God's and Pete's habitual range of vision until they had forgotten about me.

Most shades I had observed remained static or just floated languidly along—no need to hurry when you've got an eternity to get where you want to go. But waiting around like sheep to be slaughtered is not the Treadwell way. I was determined to *act*.

So I told myself.

A troubling factor was that Pete appeared and disappeared whenever he felt like it, or maybe whenever God felt like it. Where he came from and where he went was a mystery. Distance does not seem to be a consideration for high-ranking divine beings, so getting away from them would be extra hard if not impossible. Thinking about that, it occurred to me that heaven is like a giant chessboard. We shades are like pawns, generally able to move only in one direction and one step at a time. I was going to say that God is like the queen, or like the queen and a knight combined. But I had to jettison that analogy because God can do what no combination of chess pieces can do: move instantly, even when it's not his turn, to any space on a universe-sized board whether it's occupied or not.

How escape then? I don't know what you would have tried, but I willed myself to appear on a cloud I observed a few miles away. It seemed to be about that distance, though my estimate might have been off by a hundred thousand miles or so. All I felt was a little shudder, as if someone had agitated my cloudlet. My next thought was, How fast can I float? To this end, I managed to levitate myself a few feet into the air. (Maybe I should call it aether, because there is no air in heaven, or at least there's never any wind, at least as far as I've noticed.) By the way, I didn't mention it—and you've probably guessed as much anyway—but you don't need to breathe in heaven. Nonetheless, shades like me are allowed to *feel* as if they're breathing, but only gently. Getting out of breath simply can't happen. Neither do angels flap their wings to get places. Not needed. Why do angels have wings if they don't need them to fly? You might as well ask why peacocks have blue and green feathers. It's basically like a logo, if you'll excuse that coarse term. True, that on those rare occasions when angels land on Earth, they may need their wings to fly, and that even if an angel is on a mission not requiring flying (the case in most instances, by the way), they need wings because people expect them to have wings.

Forgive this digression. To return to recounting my attempted escape: After failing at what I'll call instant teleporting, I simply willed myself to float fast. Amazingly, that was all it took! Clouds and extensive empty spaces passed by, and more clouds and what I thought of as signposts, lucent rays of celestial light that play through the clouds like beams from a hidden sun and imbue the scene with surprising and rare and almost incomprehensible beauty such as you may experience, even if you're mindful enough to notice, only once or twice during the course of a lifetime, if at all.

Thrilled with my new freedom, I willed up my speed until the clouds seemingly passing by were no more than blurred streaks. Of course there was no wind in my face, and I soon realized that speed was meaningless, and therefore time meaningless, and therefore distance meaningless. Heaven, like the physical universe to which it is related but not part of, is boundless in all respects.

At some point (and surely much time passed on Earth during this lacuna), I willed myself to slow down. I wanted to bring the clouds into focus as much as possible, though there's not much point to it, since they come into being blurred, remained blurred throughout their existence, and dissipate blurred.

In this case my will seemed to produce nothing. I continued floating so fast that nothing was perceivable around me but the sort of extreme blur you'd experience looking from one train at another passing in the opposite direction.

Had I condemned myself to whisking through heaven at unimaginable velocity with no prospect of encountering another being? In trying to escape, had I escaped into an unimagined variety of hell? That was a palpable fear, but it turned out that I had been slowing down without realizing it. After the equivalent of a few minutes or years on Earth I could tell by the rate at which clouds were seemingly passing—by the diminishing degree of blurriness in my surroundings—that I had slowed, and this continued until I had reached the drifty floaty speed at which shades normally proceed in heaven. Then I was gliding upward, as if toward a higher sphere, one that I imagined was closer to God.

So much for thoughts of escaping from God, but I was about to find consolation: My cloudlet was nearing a radiant female shade draped in a silken robe. I couldn't take my eyes off her. I willed myself to float slower and move closer, and soon I was so close I could have reached out and touched her, though I didn't dare—she glowed with a holy, off-putting radiance.

"For the first time I feel like I've reached heaven," I communed to her. "I could behold you for eternity and never be bored. May I ask your name?"

She smiled in a way that reminded me of one of Raphael's sublime renderings of the Madonna, and in the sweetest voice I ever heard, told me that she was Beatrice.

If air, lungs, and throat had been available to me, I would have gasped. I knew at once that this was not any beautiful woman named Beatrice, but Dante's Beatrice, who had died as a child and become the fictional Beatrice Dante encountered in heaven.

"Are you she?" I asked. "You were a real person in Italy in the thirteenth century?"

"I was a real person, and my reality in heaven is beyond any reality on Earth."

"Forgive me. Then is Dante himself here?"

"Con il suo amico Virgil." She replied, but a mist was already drifting between us. When it passed, Beatrice was gone, and I held her visage only in memory.

In motion once again, I felt another presence, this one grave and overwhelming. It seemed to pass, but I noticed that the cloudlet I was perched on was drifting closer to a darkening cumulonimbus cloud, or rather its heavenly analog, what on

Earth would be a harbinger of a severe thunderstorm or even a tornado. Lightning flickered about it, and flashes were visible within its depths. This dense, massive nebulosity was moving toward me, or I toward it, or it and I toward each other, or I was moving away from it but it was overtaking me. Impossible to tell, and that added uncertainty contributed to a feeling of dread I was experiencing beyond anything I had ever known. Heaven, it seemed, was about to be subsumed into hell!

7

The distance between me and the threatening nebulosity continued to close. From my perspective it took on colossal proportions. So massive was it and so turbulent the movements of space that accompanied it that I was swirled about as if caught in an eddy of a swiftly flowing river. I sensed that I would soon share the dark destiny of the shades entrapped in its grip.

Closer now, I realized that what had appeared to be a single great cloud was composed of countless small, dark gray, almost black, cloudlets, each "supporting" a ghostly figure, a shade who, I speculated, had fallen into God's disfavor and for some reason been lodged in this forsaken corner of heaven. I prayed (prayed in heaven!) that this aggregation of doomed souls would pass without enveloping me its midst.

Drawn closer still, among the cloudlets closest to me I observed shades so benign-looking that I wondered if they had been assigned by mistake to this congregation of the damned. Some began breaking away from the central region, and fortune carried me toward them. I watched the others with foreboding as they disappeared within the dark nebulous mass, their destiny forever to remain a mystery.

Examining the faces of those who had broken free and were

passing close to me, I was astonished to see the shade of Jeff
Clay, a good friend during college years who had been stricken
with a rare form of leukemia and died when he was only forty.

"Jeff!" I communed to him, concentrating my thought with
maximum intensity and with as precise directionality as
possible.

I was delighted when I saw that he recognized me. A shift in
the aetherial current freed him from the cluster of shades he
had been accompanying, and his cloudlet drifted close to mine.
My spirits soared. Jeff was the first shade I'd encountered I felt
I could talk to freely. Presumably he had arrived in heaven soon
after he had died and had been here close to forty years, long
enough, I hoped, to unravel some of its mysteries.

Jeff was as surprised to see me as I was to see him. Instead of
discussing our urgent concerns, as we should have, we started
talking about adventures we'd had during college years. We had
barely kept up with each other after graduation—I had gone to
work teaching at a private school in Brooklyn and Jeff had
attended Stanford Business School, then joined a consulting
firm in San Francisco and was on his way to big time success
when he fell ill. I had a phone conversation with him a month
or so before he died. He never mentioned what I learned later
he knew then: that he had little time to live.

Belatedly I realized that I should be trying to find out what
he knew about heaven. Like other shades I'd encountered, he
might disappear at any moment.

"It's just incredible what's happened to me since I got here,"
I communed. "Have you heard that God is depressed?"

"I have. If that rumor is true, it's very spooky."

"It's the only reason Saint Pete hasn't judged me." I said.
"He has such scary mood swings, I don't know what to believe,

if anything! But first tell me this, if you know: *Are* we in heaven, or in hell, or something in between?"

"I thought you might ask that," Jeff said. "It's a question I'm not sure I can answer. I almost asked you."

"But you've been here forty years. You must have gotten some clues. Did you talk to Pete much?"

"Only when I first got here. I thought I'd be tossed into hell without a trial."

"How come?"

"You don't know? When I broke up with Mary—we'd been married about six years—it was just a cold calculation, though I didn't advertise it that way. Mary was pleasant enough, but dull, and Kitty was simply more beautiful, smarter, more accomplished, and crazy about me, and so I just walked out. I told Mary it was because we couldn't have kids and didn't want to adopt any, a completely phony reason."

"Ugh. No good," I said, "and it's something like what happened to me, or rather what I caused to happen to someone because of me, Sue Marcello. You never met her, but in your case, well, that was pretty bad, but you made up for it in a lot of ways I bet. When we had that last phone conversation you said you'd been tutoring disadvantaged kids. I bet it made a big difference for them."

"Yeah, but there were other things I did wrong. I was in an investing group and got some information and bought stock in a company through an agent. It was a deal where I had a moral obligation and maybe a legal obligation to bring it into our group, but I didn't want to share this big gain on what amounted to a sure thing. I told myself it was making up for how one guy was already too rich for his own good and another was getting too big a management fee, which he was, and I was pretty sure that the other guy in our group had already done just what I was thinking of doing, so. . . . Anyway, I had a theory as to why I didn't have an obligation to share it, but I was just kidding myself. I *knew* that, but I tamped it down in my subconscious. It seems incredible to me now that I could have behaved in such a way, and with Mary. Well, it's not worth talking about. The point is that what I'd done was pretty bad. That became painfully clear to me but not until I got here."

"Did you do anything to compensate for it?"

"You could say that. It wasn't intentional. It was just a few weeks after I cashed in on that deal and became the owner of an offshore bank account. I started feeling sick—it came on fast. I was diagnosed, told I had about six months at best without chemo and maybe a year with it. Was that ever a clear message! So I made up for what I'd done in that sense, and then more after I died and got to heaven. And even before seeing Saint Peter it hit me: I had an epiphany—I saw my whole life and my behavior in a different light. I couldn't believe that I'd been the person I was, and I still feel that way. It's just incredible the difference in perspective. When I saw Saint Pete, I said, no defense, send me to hell."

"Jesus, you didn't!"

"I did. I felt that much remorse. But Pete said he'd talk to me later, and I haven't seen him since. I've been wondering all this time—you say it's forty years, it could be forty centuries for all I know—I've kept thinking at some point he would come and say the hell with you Jeff Clay."

"I feel for you. Forty years. God, that's a long time. Have you gotten so you feel better about what you did, come to terms with it?"

"Not feel better. Beginning to come to terms with it, I think.

I'm seeing it more as part of the whole great tragic comedy or comic tragedy of the human species, even of the universe. As for whether we're in heaven or hell or somewhere in between, I can't say. But my existence here has been nothing like what it was on Earth and nothing like what I thought heaven was supposed to be. At least, as you can see, thank God, there are no flames leaping up around us."

"So far, but I keep looking over my shoulder. Anyway, Jeff, the great thing is that you're here and so far you've been safe. I hope to God it stays that way."

We reverted to more reminiscing, preferring to talk about fun we'd had when we were young rather than the peril we were in now. Eventually our conversation about good old times wound down. Jeff communed:

"It's great we ran into each other, Jack. That this sort of thing can happen is a good feature of heaven."

"Agreed. Even with this personal tragedy, this feeling of remorse, you must have learned a lot and grown in wisdom."

"I hope some. I think I have a ways to go. Maybe another forty years. But how about you, Jack? What's it been like since you got here."

"Not great. I've been through the wringer, I'm suffering from overload. Unless I've totally lost any sense of how much time has passed on Earth since I died, I've been here the equivalent of only a few hours or maybe days or weeks. Sleep doesn't happen, does it?"

"Not like we had on Earth, but there are periods of unconsciousness I think, though you can't measure how long they last and there's no pattern to it, no night and day, but go on."

"Yeah, well, I've been incredibly confused. I'm waiting to be judged and the only reason I haven't been yet is that—this is what Pete says—God is depressed."

"That's what I've heard. It's hard to believe, though," Jeff communed. "If true, it's a very major event. God has reason to be depressed. Big things, very, very big changes, could happen because of this, but there's no way we can guess what."

He drew closer. We looked off at another giant dark cloud. I had a feeling that it was composed of cloudlets most of which harbored shades of miscreants with varying degrees of venality.

"Huh," I said, "at this distance, what looks like a great solid mass is probably composed of thousands of cloudlets, what I imagine a giant school of krill might look like if you were flying low over it in an airplane. I've read that a school of krill can form a bulging disc over a mile in diameter. How many krill might be in that disc, moving in accordance with some law of biology, just as billions of stars in a galaxy, in every galaxy, are moving in accordance with laws of physics?"

"Jack, your mind is drifting," Jeff communed. "Stay with me, old buddy. You were telling me what happened after you got here."

"Sorry. Yeah, first of all, when I was alive, I didn't think there was such a thing as heaven, but when I found there was, or so it seemed, I thought it would be like—you know—the official church doctrine, with hell and maybe purgatory; but Protestants don't have that, do they. I've only been here a few days; at least I think it's days . . . I can't be sure; but there are all types here. It's like nothing I could have imagined. I feel good, I feel amazingly young, I don't miss not having bodily functions. It's good floating around."

"I agree. Lot of good things, but incredibly confusing!" Jeff noted.

"Yeah, nothing more confusing than Saint Pete. I don't understand why God hasn't replaced him. There must be lots of other saints here. The idea that God is depressed is beyond strange. And further on the downside, I feel rotten as I never have before about a lot of things I did in life, and I'm scared to be judged. The possibility of an eternity in hell is very, very heavy. I guess you've felt that as much as I have."

"Damn right. I know how you feel, old buddy. I still don't get it, even after the forty years you say it's been since I died. I would have guessed about a hundred and forty. Anyway, this is what I've picked up from various cherubs and other old hands: If we had arrived here two or three hundred years ago, or more—actually any time after Jesus—heaven probably would have been more or less what people on Earth thought it was, but at least for as long as I've been here, and I'm sure a lot longer, there have been signs of change. It began with signs that God was becoming less sure of himself, or maybe he was becoming more experimental, changing instructions he gives Pete, and that disturbed Pete, who seems to be totally loyal to God but doesn't strike me as particularly bright, although, God knows, he's knowledgeable. Anyway this seems to have escalated into a crisis. God may be having a full-blown nervous breakdown, which I don't say disrespectfully. Believe me, I'm respectful to everyone, even the miscreants I run into who ought to be in hell and not floating around here."

"Yeah, that's my take on what I got from Pete— a nervous breakdown. But I don't think that term is used by psychiatrists anymore. They talk about mood disorders, depression, anxiety, that sort of thing."

"Whatever they call it, we have a pretty good idea what God has. Clinically I think it's still called depression."

"Yeah. I guess so. Under normal religious doctrine, instead of getting depressed, God would have caused another flood like what happened in Noah's day."

"I don't think he would want to drown seven billion people just to save new Mr. and Mrs. Noah."

"Hope not. Jeff, do you think you're going to be judged? Are we damned? Or have we already been? Do you have any idea what your status is?"

"I don't think I have a status, even after what you say is forty years. Maybe I'm a close case and they are still thinking about it. Forty years seems like a long time to us, but to God it's probably like a few seconds."

"Even less. Microseconds. I'm thinking of the ratio of a human lifetime to the lifetime of the universe. Still, I wish they'd hurry up and decide my case. This waiting around is hell."

"Hell is much worse, Jack. Believe me."

Jeff's last remark gave me a feeling that he knew something I didn't, and I wasn't sure I wanted to find out, so I communed nothing back. We floated silently for a while, each immersed in his own thoughts, then I asked:

"How bad do you think our sins were? Were they over the top?"

"Speaking for me, in an absolute sense, yes. In a relative sense, relative to the average person, I hope not."

Again we lapsed into silence, I wouldn't know whether for minutes or years. Heaven, I was beginning to suspect, was not so much a place where time didn't pass, as one where it simply didn't count.

Jeff resumed:

"You know what my biggest mistake—call it a sin, if you like—was?"

"No, but I'll tell you mine. I didn't appreciate what I had. I didn't appreciate life."

"I appreciated life too much. I kept grabbing for more. I was grabby," Jeff said. "Was grabbiness one of the seven deadly sins?"

"Something like it, I think. Coveting?"

"At least we feel rotten about ourselves," Jeff said. "Maybe we'll get credit for that."

"Assuming God is depressed," I said, "do you have any theory about how he's likely to act?"

"I've been thinking about that while we've been talking. I don't know much, but I'll tell you what I do know, or think I know, or at least what—"

Jeff never got to commune what he was thinking of. Instead we watched dumbly as a dark iridescent formless mass appeared and grew until it dominated all space around us, then grew larger still and darker, giving way to stupendous thunderclouds from which lightning streaked in all directions. Suddenly all space was suffused with white light; then it returned to its normal delicate blue appearance, and a sonorous voice lodged in my mind, not only in my mind, but everywhere in my being. The effect on me was beyond description. I knew without doubt that we were in the presence of God himself, and that he was about to speak.

8

I, Lord God, creator and divine ruler of the universe, am unhappy about the Virgo supercluster of galaxies, particularly the Milky Way galaxy, particularly the Earth. Earth's felicitous size, composition, proportions of elements, position relative to its sun, character of its moon, and abundance of water were close to perfection. The eons when life evolved and spread out across its oceans and the first one-celled animals appeared were some of my happiest since I brought this universe into existence.

I watched with pleasure as an enormous variety of species spread over the planet, evolving into ever more diverse forms. I marveled when mammals appeared, then hominids. I was thrilled to watch early humans begin to develop their languages and speculate about the nature of reality, learn to control fire, and hold their own against predators.

Then they began to speculate about me, or what they claimed was me. I knew that it was natural for them to imagine that I must exist and created the universe. The universe to them was no more than the Earth, sun, moon, planets (which they called wandering stars), and those true stars that were visible to them, which many thought to be fixed in a crystalline dome over the globe. Later, when some realized that the Earth was not the center of the universe, persons claiming to speak on my behalf scoffed at them and persecuted them. That bothered me.

In every culture on Earth humans made up stories about me—how I caused droughts and floods and pestilences (a charge that would have amused me were it not so insulting), then set up rules they said fellow members of their clans were obliged to follow or I would punish them.

Some people referred to me as the Great Spirit. That was closer to the mark. I was heartened by the life and teaching of Siddhartha Gautama, a fellow who, though sadly he was life denying, had good instincts about the interplay of life and the cosmos. But those tribal religions! Whatever tribal society I looked in on, I'd see priests assuring their fellows that they were the chosen ones, that only their version of me was true!

They claimed that I had selected their tribe or cult for special favors and special punishments about which only these priests could speak with authority. And this baleful practice is still going on! Oh how I've hated this false righteousness, this begging for my favors, this cant, this self-serving piety.

The oddest thing these priests told their people is that I did all kinds of cruel things out of spite. In one case they claimed that I told one of their leaders to kill his son just to please me. What blasphemy. In almost every variation of religious "faith," priests and rulers shunned those who thought I was more like I am, a spirit suffusing the universe. Shunned them, stoned them, and tortured them. They spoke of faith, hope, and charity, but what I witnessed most often was greed, lies, and cruelty.

Jesus came into the world. The calumny that I would create a human son (as if I would want to), then arrange for him to be tortured to death was the worst blasphemy of all.

The Crusades, the Inquisition, centuries of religious wars, enslaving populations, mass murders, some of which priests and religious leaders claimed I instigated or approved. Cruelty to people. Cruelty to animals. Offering prayers. Asking forgiveness. Why should I forgive anyone and what difference would it make if I did? Whatever it is someone has done they regard as sinful, they should be trying to make up for it and avoid doing it again instead of beseeching me for forgiveness. Prayers, creeds, rituals, chanting, "Glory to God on the highest. Let us bow down before the Lord." So craven, so often meretricious and malicious.

From the time humans first walked on Earth I've seen countless selfless acts in every culture, in every era, acts of kindness and good will that delight me more than any mortal could know. I had reason to hope that the faculty of reason would enable humans to attain a plane of existence where honesty, empathy, and compassion would be the linchpins of their behavior. I thought the Enlightenment and the development and acceptance of the scientific method would raise humans to a more noble place in the universe.

Yet, despite the accomplishments of science and the bringing the scientific method to bear on their problems, despite the magnificent creations of art, music, and literature, despite the brilliant ideas of philosophers (excluding the crackpot brilliant ideas), despite the hundreds of millions of acts of kindness that occur on Earth every day, and despite my regard for human beings as one of the most astonishing and impressive species in the universe, or at least in their supercluster of galaxies, more and more they resemble cancer cells, growing ever more out of control, spreading over their planet, threatening to choke it and hence themselves as so many of the richest and most powerful among them grasp for ever more power and wealth.

HAVING UNBURDENED HIMSELF and without bothering to repeat the special effects he had displayed on his arrival, God vanished, leaving Jeff and me shocked and apprehensive.

I had listened to God's lament with awe and respect, also with alarm. I could understand his feelings. There was surely much justification for them. But, and I don't mean to be disrespectful, there was something ungodly about his performance. His rant—to be honest that's what it was—seemed to confirm that he was indeed having a nervous breakdown and was clinically depressed.

I could tell by Jeff's expression that he had been much affected.

"Holy Mary mother of God!" he exclaimed, thereby reminding me that he had been brought up Roman Catholic, then abandoned the faith. "That was the weirdest thing— beyond weird—I ever imagined. I'm beginning to have some understanding of God's state of mind."

"I wonder if he broadcast that all over heaven," I said.

"What did you think of it, Jack?"

"It was quite moving," I said. "But God *is* God, after all. If things aren't working out the way he hoped, shouldn't he be able to take it, or maybe I should say, not take it so personally?"

I could sense Jeff's extreme distress as he communed:

"I don't blame him, considering human history, magnified in the last hundred years by ever increasing population pressures, more destructive weapons, torture, cruelty, people butchering each other, despoiling the environment. Imagine how he feels, watching all this in *his* universe? When we were alive, we mostly read news reports or saw footage of crimes on television or, I guess in your case, a lot was on the Internet, right? God sees it all, every single event as it is happening all over the world! He could have stopped it, but that would be turning humans into automatons. Is freedom worth it? It's a close question, in my opinion."

"Maybe, but still," I said, "at first I thought it might be good for God to be get all this off his chest, but it was scary the way he built up steam as he went along. Like a volcano that starts rumbling, then smoking, then . . . *cancer cells spreading over the planet!* If God blows, he could destroy the Earth and take the rest of the universe with it!"

I had a feeling Jeff wasn't listening. He continued: "It's been a terrible disappointment for him having people act the way they do."

"But he might have focused more on the beautiful accomplishments of the human species. He acknowledged that, but pretty skimpily. He could have said more about great art and music, architecture, science, engineering, and more about heroic acts of kindness and selflessness. I think he should have given humans more credit. We deserve a chance."

It only occurred to me as I finished communing this to Jeff that our thoughts might not just have been exchanged between ourselves, but also reached the mind of God. We thought he had left us, but since he could be everywhere at once, he may not have. I said nothing to Jeff about this, and the two of us perched motionless, silent upon our cloudlets, lost in our thoughts, humbled and bereft of any notion as to what to do next.

"I'm trying to see human history from God's point of view," Jeff said after a while. "It seems he kept hoping that humans would shape up because they had the gift of reason, and he was excited by the Enlightenment, the advent of the age of science. He must have been pleased as punch with the discovery of DNA, like a parent whose kid is in a treasure hunt and the kid figures out a clue and is the one who finds the treasure. I can understand how God loved watching the investigations of great scientists and tracking their thinking. But the arrival of the age of reason didn't stop people from being cruel to each other. The bloody course the French Revolution took must have bothered God a lot. Napoleon. And they make him a hero! Human history is essentially the history of warfare. The twentieth century was just appalling, and the twenty-first may be even more so. So many monsters taking control of so many countries; greed, avarice, corruption, and cruelty on a mass scale. The central message of what God said is pretty clear. Humans have generally acted badly and show no signs of shaping up. That was true even when I was alive, and there's been more of it since, with more chance of maniacs getting hold of nuclear weapons."

"True, there's a serious danger of cataclysmic events," I communed, influenced by Jeff's passionate reaction. "Look at how dictators have been hacking away at their own people in the Middle East and in Africa."

"And elsewhere. Look at the U.S.—what I think Lincoln called 'the last best hope on Earth.' Instead of people getting more enlightened, there's been what a cherub I know calls 'the cultivation of ignorance.' "

"But, still, don't you think God's view of things is, well, a bit extreme."

"Billionaires financing elections."

"I, know, it's sad, Jeff, but—"

"More than sad: Using up Earth's resources, polluting it, raising sea-levels; no thought of future generations."

"These are big problems, but technology is advancing so fast, there's a good chance that—"

"The U.S. is becoming a dysfunctional plutocracy. That's straight from a high-ranking angel I talked to. What's more—"

I didn't get the rest of what Jeff was trying to commune to me because we were drifting apart and neither of us had thought to alter the course of our cloudlets. Jeff had either gotten out of communing range, or maybe he just couldn't complete his thought. It seemed that for him God's reaction was perfectly rational, and I had to admit there was something to be said for that point of view.

I closed my eyes; a period of unconsciousness followed. When I opened them, I was alone. Jeff was gone, God was gone, and a grim conviction had formed in my mind that it would next be Satan in whose presence I would find myself.

9

I floated on and after a while passed a succession of unoccupied cloudlets. Were they reserved for shades expected to arrive soon? Or had shades perched on them been cast into hell? Or both? I was still pondering that and wondering whether each new arrival gets a fresh cloudlet or, more likely, a used one, when one drifted close to me. It was occupied by the shade of a man with a mostly bald head and a long gray beard, clearly not Satan.

"New here?" he communed.

"Yes, Jack Treadwell's my name, or was, and I guess still is."

"Treadwell. I knew a Treadwell once, Vicar of Cheriton. But you strike me as having lived more recently."

"Probably so. You look familiar, sir—I think I've seen a picture of you."

"It's possible. I understand my work proved to be of importance."

Connecting the face before me with pictures I summoned up from memory, I realized that the shade I was communing with was that of Charles Darwin!

"Doctor Darwin, if I'm not mistaken," I began. "I'm most honored to meet you, sir. Your work, along with Newton's—"

"Tush tush, no need for encomiums. You appear to have

been judged worthy of residing in heaven. In keeping with what I've been told is the modern style of address, you may call me Charles. Are you here permanently, Jack?"

"I hope so, I replied. I haven't been judged yet, I believe because of God's illness."

"Yes, I heard his lament. Apparently it was broadcast all over heaven. Unsettling to say the least, but I have great faith in God. I'm sure he will recover. And having contemplated the consequences of his creation more intently will be at his most compassionate and forgiving."

"I hope so too, sir . . . Charles."

Our conversation proceeded most amiably. Darwin didn't have to communicate audibly, of course. Like everyone else in heaven, he communed thoughts directly into my mind.

"Fear not," he said at some point. "I'm sure you will be admitted to heaven."

"Thank you, sir."

"Charles."

"Thank you, Charles. It means a lot hearing that. I wish I could stop worrying about it."

"Well, to get your mind off it, would you like to take a walk with me. I was about to stretch my legs, figuratively, as it has to be."

"I would be honored to accompany you. Where were you planning to go?"

"On one of my favorite paths through the cosmos."

"The cosmos? You mean the universe? The physical realm?"

"I do indeed."

"How do you have power to do this?"

"By the grace of God, of course. I had the great good fortune that he looked with favor upon my work. He told me that he particularly enjoyed observing me during my voyage on the *Beagle* and even apologized that I had so much trouble with seasickness. Imagine, God apologizing to the shade of a mortal being! I was touched beyond words. 'Now you may voyage through the cosmos,' he told me. 'And this time without suffering any gastric indisposition!' Isn't it wonderful that he would speak to me as if we were equals, when in fact the gap between us is almost infinite. Beyond that, he confided to me to a considerable extent about how the universe is organized and how it functions. I have become as well versed as modern astronomers! So, you can see, Jack, why I have such faith and confidence in our Lord."

I was stunned to hear this and grateful that by one of those wild coincidences, so rare on Earth, but perhaps, as I was learning, not so rare in heaven, I had been befriended by one of the greatest scientists who ever lived. "Of course, I would be most happy to accompany you," I communed.

At that, Darwin, perhaps unsurprisingly, since he had been a man of tremendous energy, took off at a rate I thought I could never match, having forgotten for the moment how effortless traveling at any speed is in heaven.

So it was that, for what might have been comparable to a few tens of thousands of miles, we swept past clouds, some of meteorological aspect and others that on close approach revealed themselves to be composed of innumerable cloudlets most of which were occupied by shades. Then the light that suffused this scene, radiating, it seemed, from all points above, below, and around us, dimmed until we were immersed in total darkness. I still had the sense that we were moving, but couldn't begin to guess at what speed. I strained my eyes, trying to see something that would give a hint of our location, direction, and velocity. At one point I saw a fuzzy patch of light, but it quickly disappeared. Perhaps it was a hallucination, one that I speculated might be occurring within a larger hallucination! My anxiety was relieved, however, as I sensed that Darwin was humming, happy on his stroll through the cosmos.

"Say, Charles," I called to him, feeling a bit more relaxed and familiar (perhaps too familiar I immediately thought, and would have apologized had it not seemed that it would set the wrong tone). "Where are we? Might we see the Earth down there?"

"Like from the space station new shades have told me about? Oh, my goodness no. What makes you think we're near Earth?"

"Where are we then?"

"We are approaching a point in space that it would be fair to say is at a distance from Earth equal to the average distance to Earth of all points in the universe, so unsurprisingly there is nothing you can see. Transported, as we are, to a random point in space, you're not likely see anything at all, though perhaps you'll make out a few tiny blurry patches, each a distant galaxy. It would be even more unlikely if you found yourself *inside* a galaxy, and phenomenally improbable that you would be within the solar system of a star. We'll be traveling through more densely occupied areas, however, where aggregations of galactic superclusters are quite commonplace."

"I see," I said, faking it, though I'd promised myself never to do that anymore, and quickly adding, "A question I've had: In all this vast universe are there other planets with life on them? Is our God, God of these too?"

"Yes there are, and he certainly is."

"And do some of these have intelligent life? With creatures who go to heaven or hell when they die?"

"Indeed. I have it on good authority that they do."

"Are there any here? Any aliens from other planets in heaven—our heaven—that I could observe?"

"No. I can answer that with some assurance. The world of each advanced life form has its own divine realm. I've been told that a few hundred million Earth years ago God permitted a region of heaven to form in which shades of members of intelligent species from different planets—different galaxies as it happened—could be in contact with each other. The result was most unfortunate."

On Charles and I swept through patches of space, some where we could see only faint distant stars and others resplendent with myriads of stars and polychromatic illuminated dust clouds and emission nebulae so bright that they would have hurt my eyes were not heaven a place where truly physical sensations do not occur.

Remember, noble readers, that we were spirits there, in some respects resembling living humans but without carnal appetites or sensations or the physical vulnerabilities and infirmities and indignities that are the lot of living creatures. Instead, our existence was purest thought and reflection. At least that's the ideal.

We had traveled on at far greater than light speed, the physical principle of relativity with its limitation of velocity to that of light having no application in the spiritual plane we were traversing, and nothing lay about us but scattered faint fuzzy patches of light, which we now discerned in every direction. Charles explained that they were galaxies and clusters of galaxies separated from each other by such vast expanses that mere mention of their respective distances from us and from each other set my mind churning with confused thoughts.

We zoomed in on some galaxies, then on some stars that grew in apparent size and brightness until they resembled miniature suns. A planet that looked much like Earth swam into view. Charles's thoughts entered my mind.

"Intelligent creatures inhabit that planet, ones less illustrious and accomplished than Earthlings, but far more sensible. Nearly all of them will spend eternity in heaven."

"How did they do it?" I communed. "If only Earth people could be like that!"

"The cosmos is made up of anomalies," Charles said. He did not elaborate, and I felt some hesitation in pressing him. Further on, he communed:

"Even though I have been in heaven for what seems like a long time, if there were time here, but on the cosmic scale a brief time indeed, I've been able to observe that on every planet where life exists, in each case it plays out in its own distinctive way."

"How does Earth . . . how do humans stack up against other intelligent creatures?"

"Stack up? Rank, you mean? Not well. Generally, Earthlings—humans—are in the lowest quintile. But they have created wonderful things, some of them not excelled anywhere else in our local supercluster of galaxies: music, art, poetry, architecture, some works so beautiful, God told me, that it's a great consolation for him."

"Consolation?"

"Witnessing beautiful achievements, jewels shining up from the muck of human history."

"That's a rather harsh view of humans," I said.

"I agree with you," Charles communed. "I sometimes I think God is too hard on our species, and on himself—I think this is the root of his current depressed state."

I took that in, somewhat dismayed at the idea that God thought of human history as "muck," but feeling proud that in the whole vast galactic supercluster, indeed in the entire universe, Earth seemed to be a very important planet. And, at least in the arts and music, it sounded as if humans might be in the top quintile. I had been wondering how many worlds had brought forth comparable beings, but asked a different question:

"How big is space? How far does all this go on?"

"From within our universe, it is infinite, but from outside our universe, it is finite."

"Oh, I see."

"I rather doubt if you do. I certainly don't. In any case, it's not important to us."

"I have read that our universe is actually part of a multiverse. At least that's what some of our best scientists believed when I died."

"They are correct."

"That leads to the question as to whether God rules other universes beside our own?"

"Just this one. As I understand it, each universe has its own God. Most universes are quite uninteresting. Far more often than not, life is unable to emerge because so-called dark energy tears galaxies apart even as they are forming. Others collapse within microseconds of their birth because in them gravity is a more powerful force than in ours. All sorts of factors can render a universe unsuitable for life. Imagine what it would be like if the electromagnetic force were stronger than the strong nuclear force!"

"I can't imagine," I said honestly, then, "Yet another question, if you'll forgive me, Charles. Is there a God in charge of all the others, a sort of Overgod?"

"I have heard that there is not. Everything devolves like plants that spring up from seeds, forming flowers, scattering new seeds. It is a great pageant playing out, and Gods of the various universes are tokens orchestrating the cyclic unfoldings and foldings. The life of the cosmos is like the gathering of ocean waves, which form, interact with others, and break upon the shore, each succeeding cluster of waves in its own unique configuration. So it is with the multiverse. Gods form just as waves do, emerging as orchestrators of their universes, usually remaining with them until those universes collapse or disperse. Within each universe a personified God is the omnipotent lord. Seen from outside a universe, however, its God is the distillation of a grand set of physical and spiritual laws. When the pendulum has swung a certain number of times, the clock strikes. The hour hand advances. No being set it in motion. Its design is that it was not designed."

"Was there an *original* designer of the multiverse?"

"There was none. It, and you, and I—we all evolved out of nothing."

"But how could something come of nothing?"

"In the same way that nothing comes of nothing, nothing comes of something, and something comes of something. You should understand, Jack. There are mysteries to which there may be no answers."

This was too deep for me, and I did not pursue it further.

Charles was quiet for a great while as well, and as had become my custom during such interludes in heaven, I reverted to obsessing about my failings and fears, and so said nothing more.

At some point during my travels with Charles, I felt a jolt. Without warning, we had been displaced in spacetime, I don't know by how many billion light-years. I blinked. Standing out in the black background was a most beautiful spiral galaxy. It spread across more than a third of my span of vision. I twisted so I could survey 360 degrees vertically and horizontally. Everything was black except this one astonishing object, so stunningly beautiful that I could have floated where I was for eternity and watch it rotate and swirl like a whirlpool over its hundreds of millions of years cycle, satellite galaxies revolving and reconfiguring in tandem about it, and somewhere in that mix, spiral arms numbering seven or eight or more reaching out to the edge of it, so stars seen from within them would appear densely packed along long, irregularly defined paths through space, blue and red and orange hued-areas, patches, molecular clouds with new stars forming, others soon to explode or having exploded, their debris radiating at a relatively high fraction of the speed of light, emitting radiation at all frequencies of the electromagnetic spectrum, the whole array replete with life scaled from nanometer-sized organisms to creatures larger than any ever to swim in Earth's oceans, an aggregation of life forms evolved into a multitude of shapes and performing a multitude of functions, each embodied with strategies for survival, expressing in their forms countless divergences and commonalities.

A visual image formed in my mind: a field of flowers of

extravagant size and coloration. Somewhere in that galaxy, a few hundred thousand trillion miles more or less to the left of its nucleus, and a billion billion miles more or less above the horizontal, and a few hundred or so million years removed from us in time, they wave in a cool moist breeze off the sea.

I sensed that these thoughts and visions did not form in my brain though normal processes; they seemed to have been implanted by God himself, and other thoughts and visions as well, faster than I could absorb them and organize them into proper syntax, the prerequisite for grasping their meaning; and I began to feel like Beatrice, for whom to be in proximity of God's radiance was to be immersed eternally in holy bliss, and I wondered if perhaps it had not been Charles Darwin escorting me through the cosmos, but God himself! At last, so I thought, I was beginning to understand the nature of the universe.

In the midst of my reverie, Charles, or God, if it was he, vanished. IF YOU DON'T FEEL THAT GOD IS CLOSE TO YOU, GUESS WHO MOVED. Not this time, I would have thought, had I not then resolved to try to lose my self, following Buddha's path. It was to this project that I directed my attention, gazing now at the darkest clouds I had seen in heaven, piled atop one another, fading into invisibility at some incalculable distance.

Drifting at seemingly unearthly speed in a capsule of iridescent light, I sensed that I was moving closer to them, but their distance from me seemed to remain the same, suggesting that they and I were in the same frame of reference and still very far apart.

On I drifted, accelerating. Then I was in the clear, yet clearly still in the material cosmos, this time alone, alone in black space with myriads of galaxies of all shapes arrayed in all directions, some intermingled with great wisps trailing from the edges, whole arms of galaxies ripped by interactions with other galaxies from positions they had occupied for billions of years, clusters of galaxies each containing tens of millions of vast island universes, in some cases comprising hundreds of billions of aggregations, galaxy clusters, trillions of stars.

How many planets lie within these tremendous regions? How many with life? How many with intelligent life? How many with beings, probably not resembling Earthlings— though some may, indeed many may, through parallel evolution—and possessed of comparable or greater intellects? In how many of these civilizations have individuals learned not to ravage and assail their fellow and less powerful creatures, learned not to despoil their planets? Where in all these vast arrays would one find unblemished coral reefs and crystalline water, fish of every hue and color and combination of hues and colors, luminescent sea animals, plants ranging from the microscopic spanning less than the wavelength of light to the dimensions of stately redwoods? Where on other planets are forms of flowering life that no Earthling has seen or imagined, vistas, where, if we could look upon them, we would say, "Surely, no greater beauty can be found than this."

So I wondered: Are there not many worlds upon which God looks down with satisfaction? There may be, but it is evidently in his nature that his joy in the whole of his creation fails to outweigh the sorrow he feels in contemplating Earth.

10

I had left that tremendous region we call the cosmos and returned to the spiritual realm. I cried out and imagined I had heard my voice, a cry in the wilderness, for that's what heaven had become for me. I was no more in control of myself than a gazelle in the grip of a lion's jaws. Life in heaven felt like the end of life, but didn't I go through that when I was alive?

I cried out. For whom? For God? How could I ask God to help me? It was he who terrified me.

"Never despair" is a serviceable rubric. I should have paid more heed to it, for something happened the next moment that made me think God had heard my cry. Unlikely? I would have thought so too, but inscrutability is God's defining quality. This was true even before he became unbalanced, a word I don't think too strong to describe his mental state, but the moment that thought came to me I remembered that God might be tuned to the workings of my mind. There's no way to retract a thought, so I quickly communed: "If you are listening, God, I'm sorry." Then I thought: That may not do either. *Not* using a word that would come natural to me would betray hypocrisy. I might as well be honest. I'd better be.

But to get back to how God may have been looking out for me: The reason I thought this was that I saw perched on a nearby cloudlet the shade of someone I knew who had been dead for twenty-seven years, my nephew Wally. He had been about to get tenure as a history professor when he was killed by a drunk driver. It was a great tragedy for everyone in the family. Wally was a sterling fellow. My older sister, Karen (not my younger sister, Katie, bless her, who was still hanging on at Arcadia Retirement Estates, Unit 1, when I died), said that Wally was the only perfect person she had ever known. I'm not sure I would agree with that, but if anyone could pass St. Pete's scrutiny, it was Wally.

Speaking of Karen, I had been wondering how she was. I was pretty sure her shade was in heaven. With an eternity to look for her and my wife, Ellie, I was certain I would find them. Then I remembered that I wouldn't find them if I'd been sent to hell.

Back to Wally: As I remembered him he had a rather puckish look. He was overweight. Even so, it was hard to keep up when you were walking with him. Nothing sluggish about Wally. That was true not only for walking but for talking. He could spin out more words per minute and for more minutes than anyone I knew.

I hailed him and was delighted when he recognized me and floated toward me.

"Wally!" I communed vigorously.

"Look who by the grace of God is here," he called back.

"I hated it that we lost you so many years ago," I said. "I'm thrilled to see you."

"Same here. How fare you in heaven, Jack?"

"Confused and a little scared, I'm afraid. I haven't been judged yet and don't have good feelings about what's going to happen. Any advice you can give me would be most welcome."

"Peace, control, clarity, charity, courage, resolve, and calm. All will be well. Believe on it, and you will be saved."

That might have sounded breezy to you, but it made me feel better.

"Relax," Wally said soothingly, communing a big grin, as if he hadn't really meant it about control, clarity, calm and so forth. "I was a great sinner myself," he went on, "yet somehow I'm still here. I don't think I've been judged yet, though I have a feeling that a good span of Earth years has passed since I arrived. As I'm sure you've learned, one can't get a sense of time here."

"You've been here about twenty-seven years by my reckoning," I said. "That's by how long you predeceased me. I'm so excited to see you, but it reminds me of how weird it is that I keep running into people I know or famous figures in history. It's totally against the laws of probabilities."

"So it is, Jack. And consider this: The shades of most of the most interesting and delightful people who ever lived are here. From time to time you'll meet one, and if you stay for an infinite amount of time you'll meet them all. I can only make a feeble effort to explain these tremendous coincidences, but I learned long ago that heaven is not set up in time and space the way the world of the living is. It's more like a quantum computer where you can have vast numbers of states or possible positions in potential association with each other, so if you're thinking of someone or even *should be* thinking of someone, or they are thinking of you, or, I suppose, God thinks the two of you should be thinking of each other, you can encounter each other without regard to the separation that existed between the two of you in space and time. There's no way in terms of earthly experience to explain how this could be, but in heaven, not only is God everywhere, as religious people imagine he is on Earth, but, in a sense, everyone is everywhere!"

I knew there was no chance of understanding this no matter how much Wally might try to explain it, so I proceeded to recount my experiences since I'd arrived, whom I'd met, and how I'd heard about God's being depressed and even heard his lament.

"I heard it too," Wally communed. "Extraordinary. There's no way of telling how this is going to play out. I think *we're* safe, but on Earth they'd better watch out for thunderbolts and the like."

"*I* don't feel safe here. Pete was ready to toss me into hell. Miraculously, he didn't, or I should say hasn't so far. I told him I was penitent and begged for mercy. Little good it did. He didn't give me the slightest hint that I would be spared. It's as if God has been playing cat and mouse with me."

Wally had been listening attentively. "Let's see if I can get a handle on this," he said. "First of all, I think it was a mistake for you to say you were penitent and beg for mercy. One of the rules here, if you haven't learned it yet, is don't ask God for forgiveness. He doesn't like it."

"Yeah, God said it himself, just the opposite of what I learned when I was growing up—that you had to repent and turn your life over to God."

"All wrong. God just isn't the way he's been constructed by human minds. Some of the fashioners of religious doctrine are among the biggest sinners. The long history of leading their flocks down the wrong path probably contributed to God's depression."

"I still can't absorb the idea of God being depressed, even though I witnessed it. Did you say you heard his lament?"

"Yeah, I heard it. The word is that he broadcast it all over heaven. Ironically, I think his disaffection began when people started becoming religious. The Bible riled him no end. Those ten commandments—some were all right, others terrible—and the idea of a chosen people. And sending his son to get tortured to death—to prove *what?* That God so loved the world? It's a wonder he didn't become unbalanced after Jesus was crucified. But he showed his greatness by biting his lip and hanging in there, hoping for the best, at least until recently. It's strange, Jack—it's a coincidence of tremendous mathematical unlikeliness—you've arrived here at a unique time in heavenly history. Up until modern times—think about it: all those billions of years—God's plan was unfolding fairly smoothly. Life evolved in wonderful diversity, and God was never more happy than when humans evolved and pretty soon began walking and talking, exploring the world, large numbers of people broadening their knowledge and know-how and becoming more aware of how the world works and their place in it, and—this was their crowning achievement—inventing art and science. Innovative thinking, the golden age of Greece, printing press, spread of ideas, increasing literacy, the great philosophers, Lucretius (what an amazing and underappreciated poem), Michelangelo, Montaigne, Spinoza, Kant, Galileo, Kepler and Newton, Darwin, and so on—I'm leaving out so many names; intellectual and artistic and musical achievements of the highest order; revolutions, most bad, but some spectacularly good. America's founding fathers, even though they had tremendous flaws!

"Despite all the wars and cruelty, which could be witnessed on every continent in every culture, I think developments of this sort sustained God in his faith that humans were groping their way toward a higher state, learning to sweep aside layer after layer of gauze off their eyes until finally they could see the world around them with some clarity; and although God knew that humans could never construct a perfect society—and efforts to fashion a utopia have produced some of the worst disasters in human history—he thought that by applying ever more sharpened reasoning powers, humans would make continuing progress in eradicating superstitions and religions and uniting for the common good, stamping out tyranny and slavery and creating a world as beautiful as fields of wildflowers by a fast-flowing mountain stream."

Perhaps exhausted after this poetic effusion, Wally fell silent. I could not discern his ensuing thoughts with any precision, but he seemed to emanate a deep sadness, which I think reflected the disappointment of God himself.

"I'm sure you're right," I communed, "but the idea that God hoped that humans would do away with religion when the whole idea of religion is to acknowledge God and honor him for his creation—that's something that's still hard for me to fathom."

"It was for me too," Wally communed. "But it's easy once you understand it: All those religions were based on phony arguments and inventions, usually for the benefit of those who made up this stuff and palmed it off on others. Sure there were elements in them that God liked, particularly the idea of compassion in the major religions. But the perversions! When you look at the scene from up here in heaven (not that heaven is *up*.) . . . imagine claiming that God wants women to be treated differently than men. It was bad enough that men treated women badly, but claiming that it was because God wanted it, for example that God wouldn't want women to be eligible to be priests, or even pray in the same place in many faiths, that was beyond the pale! Same for claiming that a particular religious belief countenanced discriminating against members of other ethnicities, other religions, other sexual orientations. I can completely understand God's dismay that science and the Enlightenment and the wise words of great thinkers made little progress against such casuistry, which kept surfacing again and again, spawning organized cruelty and making ignorance even more widespread than it was. I can believe that when God looked upon it he wept."

Wally was fading from my vision and from my presence in the manner I had become used to—in the room the people come and go—and though I was still seemingly supported by the cloudlet I felt I was standing on (though as an incorporeal form I needed no support at all), I once again became aware of my helpless and isolated state, and so I resumed trying to attain a deeper understanding of myself.

That I had died at a point in the history of the universe when God was undergoing a crisis was unsettling. I realized that it also presented an opportunity. If, as now seemed certain, God had become unbalanced, it increased the danger that he would act capriciously. That could result in any number of disasters. On the other hand it could work in my favor. He might capriciously admit me to heaven!

Did I really think there was a chance of that? Once again I caught myself indulging in wishful thinking in the face of the cold and brutal prospect hanging over me that at any minute (to use a temporal word that still had emotional significance for me even though the concept of ordered gradations of time ticking off was absent), God might summarily cast me into hell.

Practically from the moment I had arrived in heaven, baleful thoughts like this had hit me like brickbats, trending from some of the time to almost all the time. How I might control them I did not know.

11

It may have been desperation leading to denial of reality, but suddenly without apparent reason for it, I began to doubt that I was in heaven and that the being who I had heard say he was God really *was*, or even that I had encountered a being who made that claim! I remembered that one of the classical philosophical questions had to do with how we can know that what appears to be real really is. Bishop Berkley claimed that there is no reality. Samuel Johnson kicked a rock by way of refuting him. You can't use that test in heaven because nothing is material. Descartes claimed that he must be real because he could think! Yet, here in heaven, even though we aren't real, at least in the sense of being corporeal, we can think.

So the questions kept nagging at me: How could I be sure it was God who I had heard speaking? How could I be sure I had gone to heaven? How could I be sure that I had died?

"Be methodical," my mother used to say, and I resolved to follow her advice: to think clearly and calmly, step by step. I had already ruled out the possibility that I had been dreaming. Was I right to do so? I think so. My experiences in heaven were not the least like the indistinct discontinuities and illogical progressions in my dreams.

Might I be hallucinating? Apparently people who are having

hallucinations, whether because of being under the influence of drugs or because of brain pathology, like schizophrenia, have experiences they can't distinguish from events in their real lives. But, as with dreaming, my sojourn in heaven had been gong on too long to be a mere hallucination. What I'd been experiencing was really happening; there was no use imagining it was not. Contrary to the rock-solid conviction I'd built up during life, contrary to scientific understanding, I was forced to conclude that there *is* an afterlife, and that I was experiencing it at that very moment.

Ah, but so often there is another layer of the onion to be peeled back. The fact that I wasn't dreaming or hallucinating didn't mean that I might not be having illusory experiences in heaven; it didn't mean I could be sure that heaven was where I was! First of all, what I'd seen and experienced was nothing like heaven as it's imagined to be on Earth.

Of all my uncertainties, the greatest was whether the person I had heard talking, who had said he was God, really was. He cut an impressive figure. He could seemingly command clouds to appear, lightning to flash, and so forth, but what if he was only a master of special effects, a sort of Wizard of Oz in heaven or in some other afterlife realm? I gave this idea its due and dismissed it. It didn't ring true. I mention it now only by way of reporting how I tried to examine and reexamine every conceivable theory as to the true nature of what I'd experienced.

It was strange territory into which I had wandered. The question was how to deal with it? I could only think of the principles one should apply on Earth: I couldn't remember everything on Wally's list, but I think his precepts were pretty much what I would have emphasized: Be calm. Think clearly. Be courageous. Be kind. Be strong. And, as on Earth, I tried to strengthen my resolve by repeating Churchill's "We shall fight on the beaches," and "We Treadwells are made of sterner stuff."

After I completed these anguished ruminations, there occurred a lacuna in my memory of events, but I think it was about then that I was floating along on my cloudlet, feeling surprisingly sprightly and hopeful the way you might think one is supposed to in heaven, my fears ebbing, telling myself that things would work out and thinking about how repeating Churchill's and father's words had been helpful, when I observed a cloudlet coming toward me, a light gray one, more fluffy than usual. As it approached, I realized that Jeff Clay was perched on it. I was surprised and delighted to see him again so soon. He braked (if that is the right word for a rapidly slowing one's heavenly motions, and therefore one's cloudlet) and in a snippet of time pulled alongside.

"Jeff! How is it going? Any news?" I asked.

"You bet there is, or at least a rumor of news, according to a cherub I've been communing with. Apparently God has given Pete full authority to judge newly arrived shades, and there's another rumor in circulation that he will also judge old shades like me who have been waiting around wondering what's going to happen to them for what you've told me in Earth time would be decades. Even more amazing, Pete is said to have appointed a defender to assist anyone trying to argue why he shouldn't be sent to hell."

"A defender—you mean like a public defender, a defense lawyer?"

"Exactly. He got the idea for it from a tremendously famous defense lawyer who just died. When this guy's shade arrived in heaven, he gave a stirring speech to Pete as to why he should be admitted. His name is Lawton McComber. I'm sure you've heard of him. He passed away and arrived here two days shy of his sixtieth birthday, bitten by a rabid raccoon, if you can believe it."

"How weird. Or not. He was pretty rabid himself."

"Maybe that was why he was so effective. He saved so many celebrities from ending up in the slammer that he became a celebrity himself. I got a good line on him from the shade of a federal judge who just arrived here; she said she knew McComber well."

"I can't believe Pete would let him in. From what I heard, his whole life was a series of shady dealings and hanky-panky on a scale you and I could never dream of."

"I think that's pretty much true. But from what this judge told me, he was incredibly eloquent. He charmed the socks off jury members, particularly females. Silver-maned, silver-tongued, one of the great legal minds in the country, and a psychologist, which may explain his success more than anything."

"I imagine so, but could he charm his way past Pete? That would be hard to believe. Con artists must arrive here by the thousands every day. I bet Pete's heard every pitch in the book."

"Here's the thing, Jack. He didn't convince Pete that he wasn't linked hand and glove to Satan throughout his life. It's hard to believe that Lawton McComber won't go to hell eventually. But he did get a stay of execution, so to speak. He convinced Pete that God is just, which means he wants justice, and that recently deceased people—new shades—who were coming before Pete often weren't able to defend themselves properly, and that it was unjust not to provide them with a lawyer to present their case, and that of course he, Lawton McComber, would be glad to serve in that capacity."

"Wow. Some chutzpah."

"Lawton Chutzpah McComber is his name. But it worked. Pete told him—the shade of this judge I talked to who arrived about the same time, and she was watching, and these were Pete's exact words—'McComber, you are going to hell, and nothing you say is going to change it, but on a temporary basis I'll let you stay here to defend new shades and help them make a case as to why they should get into heaven.'

"McComber said, 'All right, but not more than one new shade per what on Earth would be a week, and I need what on Earth would be a day with whomever I'm defending to prepare the case, and I want to be able to play golf three times a what on Earth would be a week. I'm sure you can set up a top-notch course like Pebble Beach, or even better like the Jack Nicklaus-designed course I liked to play on in North Carolina. Since heaven is supposed to be blissful and God is supposed to be omnipotent, there can't be a problem with this.'"

"Jesus, why didn't McComber ask Pete to throw in the sun and the moon?"

"He would have if he'd thought it would help his case. I think he thought he might actually get the golf course. There's not much he didn't get his way about on Earth. But Pete has had a lot of experience, a couple of millennia to be precise, and he's no pushover. He said, 'No way, McComber, you'll spend all your time, no breaks, defending new shades. It won't be an easy sort of existence, but it's a hell of a lot better than being in hell. So take it or leave it, and if you leave it, it's down the chute with you.'

"Well, can you imagine? McComber, who, as I said, was used to charming the socks off anyone he's talking too, hung his head as if to acknowledge defeat, which probably he didn't feel at all. It was a classic McComber tactic. You can bet he was pleased as punch to stave off being thrown into hell, where he knew damn well he ought to go without ceremony in what on Earth would be a microsecond or two. He's probably scheming how to work this into a permanent job and avoid hell completely. He won't get any vacations, but according to my new friend, the judge's shade, this is what he likes best, being a defense lawyer. So this bastard may have beaten the system!"

"If McComber is the defense lawyer and Pete is the judge, who is the prosecutor?"

"Pete is the prosecutor too."

"But that's not right. That would never be allowed on Earth, at least in a democratic country. It violates human rights."

"It's not as bad as you might think. Pete has to adhere to God's mandate. Pete will ask tough questions and adduce the evidence against each defendant, but God willed him to be fair, so he can't go against that. At least that's my understanding. Look at it this way, would you rather have Pete as prosecutor and a separate judge and any other lawyer defending you, or Pete as judge and a separate prosecutor and any other lawyer defending you, or Pete as judge *and* prosecutor and Lawton McComber defending you? The way I look at it, it's a no brainer. McComber will probably make arguments that Pete wouldn't have thought of, or maybe anyone else. You can bet your booties: a lot more people will get into heaven under this system."

Maybe, maybe not, I thought, and despite Jeff's breezy assurances, I was already worrying mightily whether I'd be called up for trial, and what my chances would be.

"One thing more," I said, "my nephew Wally, who I ran into after I first saw you, tried to explain it, but I still don't get it.

Hundreds of thousands of people must die every day. I don't understand how Pete, and now Pete and McComber, can handle the caseload. I've got very little idea how heaven works. How can God be everywhere? How can he know everything that's happening? And Pete, St. Peter, how can he judge such numbers of people every day? Yet when I talk to him, he seems to have all the time in heaven. Another thing is: How is it that I run into people I know, like you for instance, as if heaven were a small town and if I walk around a while I'll encounter everybody in it, when actually it's vast and may contain billions of shades?"

"I've wondered about that too," Jeff communed, "and this is pretty much from what a smart shade I know—an engineer at IBM before he died—explained to me, sort of explained. Maybe this is what Wally was getting at. The general idea is that heaven is set up like a quantum computer where you can have vast numbers of states or possible positions in potential association with each other. If God thinks that two shades should be in contract with each other—*poof*. Why there you are! It's like in quantum mechanics where particles are in superposition (in all their possible positions) and then when they are observed, they decohere and are observed to be in a particular place or traveling at a particular velocity."

"Huh? Could you go through that again?"

"Sure, but you have to understand that I don't have a firm grip on this myself, and there's a hell of lot more to heaven than we can understand in terms of quantum computers, and we can't understand quantum computers, but see, as I understand it, by holding quibits, which are bits of information in superposition, you could, even if they were only the size of, say, an electron, conduct countless more calculations per second than a conventional supercomputer can. If each possible state of a particle could be a qubit, theoretically you could have a quantum computer that, if it were big enough, could process data almost infinitely faster than any computer on Earth.

"I know that's not stating it accurately technically, but the basic idea, as I understand it, is that particles only decohere— deliver information—when they interact with other particles, which happens when you observe them. I don't think I'm explaining this well, but all you need to know, the idea is, that God, and Pete for that matter, are like giant, universe-sized quantum computers. Then too, there's the fact that time doesn't work here in heaven the way it does on Earth. That plays into it. You can think things are progressing at the rate time passes that you're used to from Earth, but they aren't."

I appreciated that Jeff was trying to answer my question. What a trouper. But all I could take from this was that God has at his command some technology so advanced that humans could no more understand it than a dog could understand the *Sunday Times* crossword puzzle, so I just said: "Thanks for filling me in, Jeff," and he gave me what I'd swear I could feel as a pat on the back.

12

As I've said probably too many times, time is immeasurable in heaven, so it might have been like for days on Earth and it might have been like for years that I drifted among clouds and cloudlets, feeling surprisingly good not only from a bodily, sensual standpoint, but also my mood was, as they sometimes say on Earth, elevated, all the way to heaven you might say; and beyond that, I felt imbued with a feeling of contentment, a feeling of certainty that I would never grow bored or tired of my condition. I had begun to imagine that I had passed the test: that I really was in heaven and was there to stay.

Was that a deliberate trick of Pete's to give me a taste of heavenly bliss in order to intensify the pain, to sharpen the anguish I would feel upon recollecting what a miscreant I had been so often in life? That speculation was powerfully reinforced when I heard a voice, sonorous and deep like Tom Brokaw's, only with more of an edge to it and even more authoritative, call out: "Jack Treadwell." Then, after a pause, "Come forward."

I whirled around, and before me, though he was no more corporeal than I was, stood an imposing male shade whose identity I recognized from having seen his living presence on television—the famous trial lawyer Jeff and I had been talking about: the great or notorious, whichever you prefer, Lawton McComber. I felt electrified, as nearly everyone did when they came into his charismatic presence on Earth. At the same time I knew that he would not have appeared and called my name unless my trial was at hand.

McComber was known for not wasting time on pleasantries, and didn't bother with any for me. No smile, no greeting, no words of encouragement, just: "Before we prepare your case, be aware how painful this is for me."

"I'm sorry for that," I said. "I'm grateful you have such empathy for me."

"It's not that, Treadwell. It's that I'm providing legal services that on Earth would command a very substantial fee, being of a quality that since my passing, is unobtainable there; yet in this jurisdiction I'm obliged to represent you pro bono, though, reviewing your file, I see nothing about you that would suggest you deserve such accommodation. But that's the way it is, and I won't belabor the matter. Now, respond truthfully and don't try to think how to phrase your answers."

My renowned counsel thereupon unleashed a series of questions, probing everything I had done or failed to do that now seemed wrong. Like a skilled dentist drilling out rot, McComber extracted every seamy, smarmy, unseemly transgression I had ever committed. Inwardly I screamed from the pain of having my core character exhibited in the bright light of truth. Every corrupt and mindless working of it was exposed in the course of McComber's interrogation. I could only pray that the two of us were truly alone. If God or Pete were listening, any last flickering chance of escaping damnation would be snuffed out. Can one rely on attorney-client privilege of confidentiality in heaven? It seemed unlikely.

Defenseless against McComber's probing, I unearthed numerous long-repressed memories of derelictions. So many were there and of such magnitude as to convince me that there was no chance that a divine judge would excuse them. Moreover, I felt so terrible, so anguished, so remorseful about this ever-growing list of transgressions that if Pete had appeared before me that instant, I think (though I acknowledge it would have been madness) I would have pleaded guilty and stood ready to be dispatched to hell.

After he had finished questioning me, McComber paused, I assume to consider what I had said. I tried to gauge his face, eager for some intimation of my chances, but like the great poker player he had been, his expression revealed nothing. (I had read a magazine profile of him that said that, though he played poker infrequently, he invariably walked away from the table richer than he had been before.) I formed the conviction that he was negatively disposed toward me, though so energized was he, so seemingly capable of throwing any interlocutor, even a divine one, off balance, that I preserved some slight hope that he could save me from hell.

I can't report how much time elapsed while I waited for McComber to give me his opinion, but I remember during this painful interim thinking that he would surely attempt to bolster my confidence and let me know how he would bring his genius to bear on my behalf. Certainly he would guide me as to what questions I might expect and as to when I should volunteer a statement, perhaps elaborate a point, and how I should recognize questions I would do better to duck, looking to him to lodge an objection. Instead, he only motioned for me to follow him.

"Come along," he communed gruffly. "You're next."

"But you haven't given me any guidance!"

"Relax, be natural," he said, and we floated in silence thereafter to the space reserved for counsel and client. Of course I had no sense of how long we traveled, either in distance or in time, but I remember that we reached an empty area with pale pink clouds billowing around us. This was evidently the heavenly equivalent of a courtroom. Pete appeared at once. He mounted a slightly raised and thicker-than-average cloudlet in front of us, bowed his head, and maintained this posture long enough so that I glanced at McComber to see if he was bowing too. He was not. I attempted to adopt an intermediate posture, a not overly pious half bow.

Next! Proceed, counselor.

Pete communed this command in an aggressive tone, which I thought inappropriate in view of the relationship we had established. No one listening would have imagined that he had confided to me about God's illness and given me a personal tour of a region of heaven. For all any observer would know, I was just one among hundreds of thousands of shades about to be judged that equivalent of an Earth day.

I think you'll agree that I had a right to feel special as far as Pete was concerned, yet his haughty mien was what you might expect if a serial killer stood in the dock. It reminded me of a technique of abusing prisoners I had read about. You treat them harshly, then gently to soften them up; then they suffer all the more when you resume your abuse. It seemed that Pete was employing this tactic with me: good cop / bad cop, playing both roles. And now, despite the presence of the great Lawton McComber, I had to face the hard truth that Pete was both judge and prosecutor.

I felt a chill coming over me, which though necessarily

emotional rather than physical, brought back memories of times I had experienced bitter cold on Earth. My previous relationship with Pete meant nothing. Anything I might say in my defense would mean nothing. I was the defendant in a show trial! Within me, I uttered a cry: *Pete, why do you look at me like that? Why have you've prejudged me?*

I tried to hope that Lawton McComber might work his magic. But how could he, having given me no guidance as to how to testify? Even as these thoughts coursed through my mind, I knew that, invested with that power by God, Pete was aware of, and was probably reviewing, every detail about my life. His expression—not exactly on his face, but in his aura, which was more manifest than any facial expression could be— bespoke the judgment he would render. I glanced at my renowned counsel. I needed his help desperately, yet he gave every indication that he couldn't care less about my fate.

I studied Pete's appearance for some indication of his thinking. Even though, like me and Lawton McComber, he was thoroughly incorporeal, he took on in my consciousness the aspect of the thin-lipped, heavy-browed, unfeeling judge I remembered from serving on a jury during a week-long product-liability trial. Perhaps for that reason he seemed to have a weightier presence, while, in my perception, McComber shrank in stature. Glancing at him, I sensed that it would strain his faculties to the utmost to preserve his renowned composure. On Earth his confidence may never have been shaken. But this was here and now, and that was there and then.

Time passed, or so it seemed, though, as I have tried to make clear, the concept is unintelligible in heaven. Or perhaps it is my memory that is unintelligible—I had endured so much, one shock after another.

At last (if I may use a phrase with such a strong and misleading, because temporal, implication), Pete communed his thoughts to me and I'm sure to McComber, and I knew then what he was thinking, what he would be "saying" on Earth: that all my life's history was spread out in the divine mind. There was no need to review it: no need to recite the charges against me, no need to summarize the evidence, or for that matter even to pronounce judgment. Nothing more was needed for heaven's business to proceed than for Pete to cause me to slip off my cloudlet and fall for a day, or a thousand days, or however long it took, until I was gathered up by the leaping flames of hell.

Pete knew what my transgressions were, and so did I, and so did Lawton McComber. A few of them raced through my mind, some appalling, others only moderately venal. I mention here no more than a sampling of ones I have not alluded to earlier in this account: I failed to stop and help an old man who had fallen on the sidewalk—the people just behind me would help him. I failed to visit my mother when she was in the last month of her life and had called to say that she was lonely—I would wait for her birthday, which never came. I lied. I boasted. I maligned an acquaintance without cause. I squandered money on vain pursuits. There were worse transgressions. The way I had hurt others now hurt me! What a compendium of misdeeds: instances of rank hypocrisy: 47; instances of thoughtlessness as to the feelings of another person: 391; Instances of sloth and self-indulgence instead of making constructive use of my talents: 267; instances of shameless dissembling: 687. Surely not that many, I thought! Yet it was precisely that number, running through Pete's mind, that now ran through mine.

Oh, what a loathsome life it depicted, and now all was held

in contemplation in the minds of Pete, Lawton McComber, and for all I knew God himself.

What next? Shouldn't McComber assert a defense as to each of my major transgressions? Should not he counter-attack, stressing the times I had been kind and thoughtful and participated in activities that conceivably might to some minute degree have made the world a less worse place? And should he not put instances of my misconduct in perspective? They should be viewed relative to the misconduct of average decent-minded people. I wasn't *that* bad! No one is perfect. We all have faults, but here is a person (me!) who tried more than the average fellow to be good! Or at least as much as average, or almost as much. Shouldn't McComber have been saying that sort of thing, only far more eloquently and cleverly and persuasively than I could?

The answer to that is "Yes." Did it happen? The answer to that is "No." Not a word, not a thought, came through from this man of whom I had heard it said more than once that he was the greatest trial lawyer since Clarence Darrow and probably better.

I was stunned, unable to understand why this incomparably gifted courtroom lawyer seemed unable to cast even one of my transgressions in a gentler light, unable to think of a single reason for Pete not to find my record (and my character) fatally blemished. Instead of hearing McComber's arguments in my defense ringing through heaven, I heard him mournfully intone, "The defense rests."

Pete, his gaze fixed on me, communed:
What say you, Jack Treadwell?

I cast my eyes down in the direction in which I feared I would soon be heading. I had been telling myself that this outcome was likely, but now that the moment of judgment was at hand I found myself totally unprepared for it. I looked desperately, perhaps reproachfully, at Lawton McComber.

The defendant evidently has nothing to say, Pete communed, it seemed to me in a gleeful tone. *Counselor, do you wish to make a closing statement?*

"I do, Saint Peter."

McComber let that sink in. One of the tactics he was famous for was pausing for an inordinately long time, a trick to raise the level of suspense. Pete, who must have imagined that the famous defense lawyer would finally offer as argument on my behalf, must have been as surprised as I was when McComber communed:

"Everything that you have charged about the defendant's behavior is true. We will deny none of it, nor will we offer any fact or argument in mitigation."

Very well, counselor. Is that all?

McComber was silent yet again, and I wish I could tell you how long it was before he then communed, "I am not finished, Saint Peter."

I had been appalled and driven beyond despair by McComber's behavior. Now my hopes began to stir, if not quite revive.

Of course, counselor. You have the right to finish your statement. But since you haven't presented any defense, there is nothing to sum up. You might as well just lie back and relax on your cloudlet.

"If I may say so, respectfully, Saint Peter," my renowned lawyer thundered, for the first time showing some moxie, "I never relaxed back on my cloudlet on Earth, and I'll be damned if I'm going to in heaven!"

Damned is the right word for you, counselor. That's just what's happening to you. Your little ruse to hang out here in heaven and avoid being sent to your more than properly deserved destination will have no further effect.

"Wait a minute," McComber communed, forgetting that there aren't any minutes to wait in heaven. Nevertheless, I was thrilled to hear his voice-like thoughts come across so forcefully and authoritatively, when moments before he had been so outrageously passive in my defense. He continued:

"I submit to you with utmost respect, Saint Peter, that our understanding was that this would be a fair trial of my client, and that includes the judicially and legislatively and constitutionally enshrined right to sum up my case!"

The trouble with that, counselor, is that you presented no case, so there is nothing to sum up.

"Respectfully," said McComber, dragging out the word so Pete could hardly miss the sarcasm in it, "there is."

If so, it can't take long, I won't permit you to speak at length.

"I don't need to speak at length. I need only make a brief point to prove that my client is entitled to be admitted to heaven."

I'll decide that, Pete communed. *Let's get this over with.*

McComber stretched up to his full height, even beyond his full height it seemed, exhibiting the almost supernatural rhetorical capabilities for which he'd been famous on Earth.

"All the sins and transgressions you've witnessed by causing Jack Treadwell's mind to entertain them and lay them bare for every divine presence in heaven to see are true, and I concede that almost any one of them alone would supply good reason to condemn their perpetrator to hell . . ."

McComber paused here as if he'd made a devastating point and was letting it sink in, while I was devoting every ounce of willpower to restrain myself from cursing him for not only failing to defend me, but even strengthening the prosecution's case. It infuriated me all the more observing Pete's delight at this turn, enjoying how he was about to send me and probably McComber to hell. Then, like a clarion call in the small hours of a dark night, a single word emanated from McComber's mind:

"*But!*"

But? Pete inquired.

"But. The shade you see before you, though he bears the same name as the person who is guilty of all these misfeasances and nonfeasances, who bears the simulacrum of the same body and who possesses the same memory traces, who by anyone who knew him would have been recognized as the person who is the subject of this proceeding, is, nevertheless, *not* the same person who committed these misfeasances and nonfeasances.

"If you'll review Jack Treadwell's actions, utterances, correspondence, emails, texts, social network postings, encounters with others, body language, and, most important of all, his most notable thoughts in the weeks prior to his death and thereafter, you'll find deeply moving proof that he felt profound remorse over his previous behavior. You know this very well, because *you* can see back through time and be cognizant of every neuronal process in his brain. You know that this is true: The Jack Treadwell before you is *not* the Jack Treadwell whose transgressions you so rightly condemn. Rather, he is an innocent and thoroughly good man."

McComber let that sink in; then in a commanding voice he communed with such force that the words reverberate in my mind even now:

"Saint Peter, acting in all honesty and with due respect for justice, you *must* admit this shade to heaven!"

In the past few what on Earth would be called days I had become more astute about the shifting shapes of beings here, and I could see that Pete's had become slightly diminished. He was clearly shaken by McComber's impassioned plea. Of course that didn't mean that he would be swayed by it, but belatedly I realized that McComber's strategy made sense. No amount of eloquence could have convinced anyone that any of my past selves should be admitted to heaven, but my present self had a chance.

Was Pete reading my mind? So it seemed, for his amorphous form loomed close to me as he communed:

Suppose you are right, counselor. What justice would there be for Treadwell's past selves? Dozens of them, by my count! Why should they escape retribution because they no longer existed at the time of his death or soon thereafter?

McComber shot back: "As you say, Saint Peter, they no longer exist, even as shades. Since they do not exist, they cannot be damned. God never set up the system so that each of the innumerable selves that each human is during the course of a lifetime would face judgment; only the one who exists at the time of judgment."

There followed one of those lacunae. I had become used to them now, instances where it seemed that time had been suspended; yet, and this is almost impossible to get across to someone who hasn't been to heaven, the sense of its being suspended didn't mean that time was passing. There just wasn't a relationship between Earth time and heaven non-time. Of course I was aware of relativistic phenomena in space such that time passes at different rates as measured by different observers, but this distortion of time in the physical realm and the absence of time in heaven are different kettles of fish. So, how long this lacuna lasted I do not know. In fact the word "lasted" gives the wrong impression because it implies a length of time of determinable duration. I can only say, if I am to be honest, that at some point (though I don't mean to imply a point in time!) Pete said:

You are a clever fellow, McComber. It is an interesting argument you have made. I'll take it up with God when he recovers from his illness."

McComber beamed at me. As far as he was concerned, Pete's acknowledgement of his rhetorical ability was the only event of any importance that had occurred. From what I knew and had seen of him, it meant nothing to him that I was still in extreme peril. What was important was that the great Lawton McComber had demonstrated once again his supreme mastery of legal advocacy.

"Saint Peter," he communed: "your public defender respectfully awaits his next case."

How do you even know there will be a next case for you, notorious sinner. Don't think you'll be staying in eternity eternally!

McComber's form shrunk toward nothingness, which I recognized at once as feigned humility.

Of course, I cared no more about *his* fate than he cared about mine. He may have been a brilliant lawyer, and Pete was obviously impressed by his argument, but my guess was that God would see it as the sort of slick piece of casuistry that was the hallmark of McComber's career. Besides, if McComber was right, it would mean that millions—maybe billions—of shades had been sent to hell who shouldn't be there. God would never admit to being fallible to even the slightest degree. To have erred on this scale would have brought his very legitimacy into question! But as I said, such considerations meant little to

McComber, maybe nothing. The workings of his mind at that moment were as clear to me as they would have been to God. He was wholly absorbed with congratulating himself that Pete had said he was a clever fellow and had made an interesting argument.

Maybe I shouldn't be so contemptuous of my lawyer's egocentricity. Through his efforts I had escaped being sent directly to hell. On the other hand, I had little cause to rejoice. I had been condemned to another period of waiting before learning my fate. I hope this is something you never have to experience. Waiting for eternal judgment is hell in itself.

13

Although Pete had acknowledged there was merit to Mc-Comber's argument, it didn't produce a good feeling in me. It was only after drifting on through heavenly space for what seemed a tremendous distance that my hopes nudged upward. The cause of this mood swing was the thought that, though I had earlier tried and failed to escape from the region I imagined Pete and God had under most active surveillance, I might be "off the radar" after all. This was such an appealing notion that it developed into a full-blown fantasy of being forgotten by Pete and God both. It was a soap bubble of a dream that burst as quickly as it formed, not because of any event, but because saner thoughts began shaping my mood. God may have become depressed, but I had to admit there was no reason to doubt that he, and Pete, with all their divine power, were fully functioning and that my chances of escaping judgment were nil.

As usual, time passed, or did it? A perennial question in heaven. If only I could have looked down on Earth and seen it rotating, I would have had the equivalent of a clock. I suppose God can, but ordinary shades like me don't have access to means of measurement of anything. By the way, I should not have referred to the Earth as being "down"—it's in another realm altogether. But what I was thinking is that I might be able to train myself to observe events, no matter how trivial, happening in sequence between two events, and by simply counting their number, estimate the time that on Earth would lie between the two events I noted; or maybe I could somehow obtain a vantage point from which I could see, or at least know about, the Earth turning in its diurnal cycle, giving me a feeling for how much time was passing *there,* and then equating it with . . . But I pursued these speculations no further. As you may have concluded yourself, they were leading nowhere. There was no way I could rig heaven so time passed, no way I could defeat eternity.

As usual, I can't tell you how long an interlude ensued, but the next thing I remember was that a shape was drifting closer to my cloudlet, a winged figure of feminine character, diaphanously arrayed and so perfectly formed that, though no trace of sensuality survives death, I experienced a sense of awareness that had I encountered such a creature on Earth it would have stirred my erotic impulses.

She came closer, and I *beheld* her, one might say, rather than looked at her. I felt that I could be happy fixing my eyes on her forever.

"Hello," I said. "I can see that you are an angel, though in beauty and radiance you exceed the vision expressed by any artist who lived on Earth."

"You may call me Juliet," she said in a tone so pure and musical that, if I could hold it in memory, my idealized notion of heaven would be fulfilled, more than fulfilled, would surpass anything beyond my imagination and I would think anyone's imagination.

It took one of those nontemporal interludes for me to

emerge from my swoon. "Are you my guardian angel?" I asked.

This brought forth the sweetest, most disarming, most appealing, most lovable laugh I had ever heard. "No," said this angel named Juliet, "but it won't do you any harm to think so."

"I am so grateful you stopped by," I said and realized at once that this lame remark would hardly commend me to her; yet I wanted to remain in her presence forever, for she was an exemplification of absolute perfection, except that her wings were tarnished, and they were pitted and frayed as if she had flown through a hail storm or endured prolonged exposure to high winds and salt spray, as perhaps she had in the course of a heroic mission of mercy, encountering terrible perils the nature of which I would never know—my dear sweet Juliet would be too modest to talk about them.

"Is there any way I can help you?" she asked.

"You are so lovely. I would do anything to help *you*." I said.

Again she laughed, this time so prettily that I wanted to prostrate myself at her lovely feet. So smitten was I that I almost forgot what peril I was in, or even where I was. Gradually, though, awareness of the gravity of my circumstances returned to my consciousness: I needed help. I was at grave risk of being sent to hell!

The image of Juliet was so entrancing I feared that, like some ordinary mortal who beheld a goddess, I would be unable to speak or move, but would remain silent and if left undisturbed would be immobile forever. It was only after a tremendous effort of will I communed to her:

"It would be wonderful if you could help me, dear Juliet. I feel comfortable here, as if I still had a physical being and were in good health, alert, and well fed. My sense of having a body, or at least of not needing one, is intact, but I am anguished wondering whether I'll be committed to hell or allowed to stay in heaven. Saint Peter put me on trial. I was defended by the shade of a famous lawyer who died recently. Afterwards, Pete— Saint Peter—said he would have to consult God before deciding how to judge me. So it appears I have been granted a reprieve until God recovers from his illness. This was only a few hours ago, or a day, or I don't know how long. But time aside, this threat hangs over me, and my anxiety is all the greater because I don't understand where time—the passage of time—fits into the scheme of things in heaven, if at all."

To this poured-out plea my angel replied:

"I understand your frustration, dear Jack. I met the shade of a famous writer who arrived here what you'd call a few Earth years ago. He said that 'time is a pitched and undulating surface which only memory can make accessible.' I don't know what he meant, but I think it speaks to the way time exists and yet does not exist here in heaven, and—"

"How beautiful you are," I interrupted.

Juliet gave me the apotheosis of angelic smiles. "I would save you from hell in a hair's breadth of time," she communed, "but I have only the power to wish you well. I hope you will be saved, dear Jack, but if not, if you are cast into hell, think of me. Keep this comfort with you—that I love you and shall love you through all eternity."

Hearing this, I felt I would melt away; not just melt away but evaporate, as if Juliet were the sun itself and I had flown too close to her. Then this thought flooded my mind, and I communed:

"Oh, Juliet, hell will not be hell, if while I'm there, I think of you."

"And I shall treasure *your* love. Now dear Jack, I must be on my way."

"Juliet, if you have just another moment—I am so curious about heaven, how it works. Have you been here long? Have you ever visited Earth? I wish we could have met there."

"Many angels have visited Earth many times. I have only once and got into the most terrible difficulties. God told me he worried too much about me and doesn't want me to go back again."

"I think you would bring only happiness wherever you go."

"I think God may believe that too, but he was concerned for me."

"How long have you been here, in heaven? Would you tell me how old you are?"

Again that pretty laugh that caressed my being and made me long for her, my Juliet.

"If you like, Jack, I am as old as the Earth, but not as old as the sun. I am as young as this moment, for oldness implies a passage of time, which I have never experienced. Neither being old nor being young are things I could be."

"Of course. I'm beginning to understand. I guess, strange as it would seem to anyone on—"

"I must go, dear Jack."

"Oh, if you could stay just for a moment more. Could you tell me: I have heard that God is not well, that he is depressed. And I have heard his lament. I seem to have arrived at a time of a great crisis in the history of heaven. Do you have any idea how this came to pass and what will happen?"

"Darling Jack" (and I swooned anew at this term of endearment), "I shall answer your question as best I can. After the primordial fireball, particles condensed, galaxies formed, clouds of gas contracted until they gave forth light, and some burst, spreading heavy elements like seeds from a popped flower. They formed the constituents of planets that could nourish life, which, as God had planned, proliferated into vast numbers of forms in vast numbers of regions of the universe, and once in a great while life appeared and evolved, and in some tiny fraction of those places, intelligent beings evolved, and in some tiny fraction of these, self-aware beings capable of abstract thought and possessing complex language capabilities evolved, and in some survived long enough to discover and embrace scientific thinking and begin to control their environments, which pleased God. Earth was one of these rare planets, and humans one of these rare species, but instead of casting off superstitions and self-aggrandizing materialistic pursuits and adopting universal abhorrence of and intolerance to cruelty, even after widespread enlightenment and after wisdom flowed from the pens of great thinkers, humans too often failed to fulfill the sublime potential they were blessed with, the basest instincts too often prevailed, the freedom God had granted was in too large part exercised to evil ends, and, despite the brave efforts of countless noble beings, the collective choices of the species became fatally destructive and self-destructive.

"God wept, and weeps still. Some have said that his tears will rain down on Earth and bring on another flood, but they say so only metaphorically and pointlessly, and all the angels and saints of heaven and Jesus Christ himself are perplexed, and none knows what will happen."

"Jesus Christ!" I exclaimed. This was the first time I had heard his name mentioned in heaven. For some reason I hadn't asked anyone about him—I'd barely thought about him, though of course I assumed he was here, or would have assumed it if I had thought about him. I still remembered part of the creed I'd been forced to memorize as a child . . . *On the third day he rose again from the dead; he ascended into heaven, and sitteth on the right hand of God the father Almighty. . .*

"Can you tell me more about him, dear Juliet?"

"I can tell you that Jesus, like all of us, is of God."

I wanted to press my question, to learn more, but desperation to learn my own fate thrust other thoughts aside:

"Do you think God's state of mind, his distress, will affect how he might judge me?"

"My dearest Jack—"

I didn't let her continue, for I was overwhelmed by a conviction that Jesus would be the key to my salvation, and I exclaimed:

"Do you have any idea what Jesus thinks? Do you know where he is? Does God consult him?"

"You must talk to Jesus yourself."

"I could meet him? I would be grateful for a chance to talk to him, but how?"

"Oh ye of little faith," Juliet said teasingly. "Search and ye shall find."

She communed a thought that took shape in my mind as "aloha," the Hawaiian word that, as I recalled, means "Hello," "Good-bye," "I love you," and "See you later." Did it mean the last three of these in this case, I wondered, or just one or two of them, or nothing at all? But I had no chance to ask, for Juliet was gone, and I was drifting again through the incomprehensibly vast heavenly realm, searching for. . . . Searching? The word has no meaning in heaven. There was no place I could begin to think of going in this three-dimensional or more, time-barren, direction-barren state of existence. Maybe, just by thinking, *Jesus, I am searching for you, I will find you. My whole being is concentrated on finding you, and giving myself to you. . . .*

Giving myself? What kind of thought was that? Something I must of heard from a gospel preacher on the car radio. Ugh. My crassness and hypocrisy showing through, even in heaven. "One of little faith" indeed. But I must acknowledge it. I must be honest. Without honesty, nothingness. God / Jesus / Pete— they all can see through me. I am one of little faith, no faith, come to think of it, for I doubt if acquiring a measure of faith in heaven counts. "It's too late, baby" . . . Carole King. "It's too late." I didn't listen when told, "HURRY UP PLEASE." If only Pascal's wager worked and it wasn't too late for me to make it, and I had hurried up, but God would see in an instant that I'm just *betting* on him. *Betting on God.* As if I were in the big casino in the sky. I'd be tossed into hell. To hell with him, God would say. But maybe this isn't relevant to me. I *do* believe now, since I *know* I am in heaven. At least I think I know, unless this is all a dream, or a hallucination. I remember now—I decided that it couldn't be either of them. What's the difference anyway? Between one of them and the other and between each of them and reality?

How muddled my mind had become. I was quite composed when I was still alive, though sometimes terribly wrongheaded, maybe because I was composed, but composed of madness, composed only in a hallucination or a dream, I suppose. But I know this isn't one. . . . I repeat. I'll cling to this: Hallucinations don't last this long, and there's a reality in everything I've been experiencing that's very different from the patchy sketchy disconnected nebulous nature of dreams. This *is* happening, and I have to be sane and calm and achieve equanimity. If I act wisely and with good will, maybe I'll pass whatever test it is I'm being subjected to and stay in heaven and attain the bliss that's associated with heaven, maybe with Juliet, though it can't be earthly type bliss, I have to remind myself. Earthly bliss I must not long for, because to do so would be to board the straight-to-hell express. Instead, I shall long for some kind of heavenly bliss that, while on Earth I could never have imagined as being satisfactory and still can't, is.

14

Juliet must have put in a good word for me, for through some mysterious process Jesus materialized before me, appearing as if still alive. Garbed in a simple brown robe, he was of average stature, with straight dark brown hair that hung halfway down his neck and a casually trimmed beard. He looked young—as young as twenty. Before I could take in more, he dissolved into a cloud, or rather what was no more than the suggestion of a cloud, retaining all the while a presence of human character.

"You sought me," he communed.

"Thank you for hearing me, Lord Jesus," I said, wondering about my use of "Lord." I was thinking of the Christmas Carol I had learned at the age of four—*Away in a Manger*, where "the little Lord Jesus lay down his sweet head." I realized at once that it may have been inappropriate to call him "Lord," but I don't think it sounded offensive; then I thought of how I just wanted to say, "Help me, Jesus. Save me! Keep me from going to hell!" but sensed that to begin with a self-centered plea would set the wrong tone to our conversation. Since no other thought entered my mind, I communed nothing.

After one of those lacunae that occurs so often in heaven, it came to me that I should show that I was worthy to stay here, and I must be honest and straightforward—Jesus might be reading my thoughts. Not that I wouldn't want to be honest and straightforward anyway.

"Lord, hear our prayer," I remember everyone saying at a Roman Catholic service I attended. That's a pretty straightforward way to approach someone regarded as a deity, and not diffident, and gave me my cue:

"Lord, hear my prayer," I said, "I am a confused sheep that has lost its way. I don't know what is wanted of me or how I am to be judged." I felt a rush of pleasure communing these words—they expressed, I imagined, honest thoughts.

Jesus was silent. I thought of how people used to go to a psychoanalyst and spew out their anxieties and fears and hopes and confusions, and the psychoanalyst would relax back in his $1,495 Eames chair and stretch a bit and say nothing or maybe after a while, "And how does that make you feel?" But Jesus was not going to be my psychoanalyst, I knew that. Yet he did remain silent like one. Since I saw no indication that he would say anything more, I continued:

"Tell me, if thou would, my Lord Jesus." Yes, I kept calling him "Lord." I don't know why, though having been an atheist, I didn't consider him as *my* Lord, even though I felt that it was *he* who was present before me; then it occurred to me that if you think you are talking to Jesus Christ in the afterlife, you are an atheist no more. But I still was an atheist as far as his divinity was concerned—I thought of him just as a shade, albeit a very distinguished one, and one of course who I could not help thinking had special influence with God. So by my use of "divinity" above, I'm referring to his divinity when he was on Earth, which I'm not sure continued in heaven, or maybe it only began when he got to heaven! Forget everything I just said! I'm making no sense again. In any case, I continued:

"Lord Jesus, I would be most grateful if you would tell me what your role is here and your relationship to God and St. Peter and what you . . ." I halted in mid-sentence, so inept and stupid did I feel in inventing these questions.

Now Jesus spoke:

"Put away your preconceptions. I can neither save nor judge you. I am a presence in heaven."

"So I *am* in heaven!" I said. "I was afraid that I might be in hell or perhaps purgatory."

"Purgatory," said Jesus, "exists everywhere there is consciousness."

"I see," I said, although I didn't. "Could you tell me if everyone here is safe. I mean that there is no hell in the sense that it's talked about on Earth, and which, if you'll forgive me, I think you yourself mentioned during your life, at least according to one account I read. I mean is there a danger of my being thrown into hell?"

"Hell is created by man, not God."

Hearing this was a tremendous relief, or at least seemed to be until I thought more about it. I remembered that when he was on Earth, Jesus was known for being cryptic at times and speaking in parables. I found it thrilling to talk to him, but didn't feel I'd gotten on a sound footing. I probed further. (Probed is not quite the right word and not pretty—I'm sorry to be using it, but can't think of a better one.)

"I've always thought that this was the case," I said, "but I was wrong about there being no heaven, so I knew I might be wrong about there being no hell. But if there is no hell, isn't that at odds with what you preached while on Earth?"

"You should understand," Jesus said, "most of what I said on earth was incorrectly reported. We knew little of the world then. We had no understanding of science. I studied the sacred texts and listened to rabbis, some wise and some not, and observed that the world was rife with greed, cruelty, and hypocrisy. I tried to show people how they should live. I was deluded into thinking that the kingdom of Earth could be the kingdom of God. I was adored by some and hated by others. I was crucified. That this happened was not part of God's plan; neither did he stop it from happening. My ministry and murder was the consequence of the freedom God gave human beings, and which they exercise for good and for evil."

"Thank you for telling me these things," I said. "May I ask what you do in heaven? Do you counsel God, or comfort him? Do you think he was wise to confer freedom on humans?"

"Not only humans, but on all intelligent, self-aware species, on millions of planets in his universe; for remember that Earth and its inhabitants constitute only a minute fraction of the cosmic realm. But of all the worlds, Earth was, and even now still is, one of the most beautiful and pleasing to God. It was, and even now is, one with an intelligent species of highest potential. God has been delighted and distressed with all that has happened in his universe, but what has happened on Earth has made him grieve."

"Oh, yes," I said. "I could hear that in his lament, and I have heard what others have said about it. I can't grasp how God can watch over all these civilizations of all these millions of planets and still have time to commune with a single poor shade like me."

"God is unconstrained by time."

"Did you or someone like you appear in all civilizations on all these planets? Does every planet have a Messiah?"

"I only appeared on the planet Earth, only one time, for a

brief span, and in one place, which is now known as Palestine and as Israel. Analogous figures appeared in many cultures on many planets. I am not unique except to Earth, but it may be that not in the entire universe has more sublime art, architecture, music, and literature been created as was inspired by my life, crucifixion, and supposed resurrection."

"*Supposed* resurrection? But you were resurrected, were you not? You must have been because you are here!"

"Not in body."

"Your soul?"

"There is no such thing as a soul. I am my shade as you are your shade. I am my continuing consciousness as you are your continuing consciousness."

I wanted to ask Jesus about what it's like having life everlasting, but as this thought entered my mind, he vanished, and I sensed that I would not likely encounter him again.

Jesus had seemed wise and responsive, but the overall effect was dispiriting. I felt a chill coming over me, mimicking physical experiences I had had in life but which seemed foreign to the heavenly realm. For a moment I thought this was a reaction to Jesus's remarks; then I realized it had been brought on by a sudden fear, not of hell, as I would have thought, but of drifting through heaven, meeting other shades, having conversations, feeling no pain, feeling bliss, but bliss forever? What would that mean? Forever *anything* terrified me. No challenges, no joy. Spiritual joy I suppose. But joy is not something that can be sustained; it's a burst of feeling. Then what? Heaven, it seemed, was as vast as the universe itself; yet suddenly it felt claustrophobic. If I could have emitted a sound, I would have screamed!

. . .

Again I was alone, again worrying that I would be damned. Heaven is terrifying, I thought, but at least better than hell, unless it *is* hell. This agonizing line of thinking was interrupted by a feeling of being borne on a whirlwind, swept through space; not space in heaven, but space in the material universe, bringing to mind lines of John Keats I committed to memory one night in mid-life when my fortunes were at lowest ebb:

> Oh what can ail thee, knight-at-arms,
> Alone and palely loitering?
> The sedge has withered from the lake,
> And no birds sing.
>
> Oh what can ail thee, knight-at-arms,
> So haggard and so woe-begone?
> The squirrel's granary is full,
> And the harvest's done.
>
> I see a lily on thy brow,
> With anguish moist and fever-dew,
> And on thy cheeks a fading rose
> Fast withereth too. . . .

I broke off before reciting the most beautiful, also the most agonizing, lines of the poem, ones I could tolerate when I was alive, but were now too painful to recall.

I would not have been able to finish this dolorous meditation as it was, because God himself appeared before me—at least I imagined that I recognized him, assuming the same dark iridescent form as before. It is a strange thing that this divine phenomenon who ruled the unimaginably vast universe and was both everywhere and nowhere could also in his entire being be located in the presence of a single poor shade who only recently and tentatively had ascended from Earth and now stood before him. I almost said "cringed before him," because I felt a preparatory constriction in my muscles, or rather my muscle analogs, for my heavenly being comprised no earthly anatomical features; but then I realized that I must appear to be confident, affect to be worthy in God's presence.

What a fantastic moment! God and I alone together, although of course he was everywhere else at the same time, and perhaps manifesting himself before every angel, saint, and shade in heaven, just as he was to me.

Strangely, it was not until that moment that I realized I was weightless, or almost so. What rules of physics applied in heaven, I wondered, my mind drifting even when face to face with God, whereas before I'd seen only through a glass darkly?

I was at a loss as to what to say. Surely *he* couldn't be. Yet, I sensed no thoughts coming from him, and the two of us remained in proximity, facing each other but with no interaction, how long I could not know, but a memory from childhood came to me: parishioners in our church, singing, some on key, "A thousand ages in Thy sight are like a single day."

God must be accustomed to spending years, even millennia, even millemillennia, without moving so much as a wisp of his amorphous form, whereas I, burdened with my earthly habit of expecting something to happen every second or so, if only a fly alighting on the window pane, became impatient. I said, stupidly:

"Can I be of service, Lord?" (I almost said "your majesty,"

choking off the word as it was forming, though surely God knew this blunder was on the tip of my tongue.)

This amorphous shape, Lord of the universe, remained silent.

"A thousand ages in Thy sight are like a single day" played in my mind, the same line repeating, for I didn't remember or had never known the ones that followed.

I waited—I had no choice. I wanted to do something, but I knew I should wait. "They also serve who only stand and wait." Milton. Even so, I had a strong urge to jump off my cloudlet, but what would that accomplish, I asked myself. So I waited, telling myself it would be fatuous to imagine that God would answer me in Earthly time, that what was happening (what was *not* happening) might be a test of my patience, which was a test of my piety, worthiness, and general admissibility to heaven. Every minute I perched on my cloudlet saying nothing tended to demonstrate that I was basically a decent shade or close enough to being one, so I hoped, but hour after hour or week after week or who knows how long, nothing happened. I couldn't stand it. Here I was in heaven, yet I was suffering! That terrible possibility revisited my mind: I might be in hell! Maybe the "God" I saw before me was an ironic illusion of that from which I was so tremendously separated. Was this the nature of divine torture?

On Earth in these circumstances I would have broken into a sweat. In heaven, where the physiological doesn't exist, the substance of my misery was compressed into mental pain so severe that I cried out, mindlessly:

"I rely on your infinite mercy, oh Lord."

This prompted a reply, though not one I would have hoped for.

15

What makes you think my mercy is infinite? If it were, everybody would spend eternity in heaven. Do you think that would be just?

"I wouldn't think *everybody*, Lord.

Whom would you exclude?

Well . . . murderers, for example.

You don't want murderers in heaven?

No, Lord. I think it would be unjust for them to have eternal bliss.

So you'd like me to show mercy only to a finite extent?

"I guess that's right, Lord."

In that case you might be sent to hell along with billions of others who lived less than worthy lives.

"Not mercy limited to that extent, Lord. I ask only that you have enough mercy to admit to heaven decent but fallible people like me, but not criminals—I mean real evildoers, of course."

Of course. Well, the fact may be that I've admitted everyone.

May be? That was evasive, the kind of cryptic answer I'd expect from Pete or Jesus, but didn't expect from God.

Don't get combative again, I told myself. Resist acting as if you've been provoked; but it would seem all right to ask a few more non-combative questions.

"Lord, if I may ask, are shades who arrive here sent to different places, depending on how good or evil they've been?"

Location has no meaning in heaven.

From then on, every question I asked and comment I made was met with an equivocal answer. When, I wondered, would this torture end? Finally, after God knows how long, I remembered something Pete had told me that might be the key!

"Lord!" I communed his holy title in a firm voice. "I have heard your lament, and Saint Peter has told me that you are depressed."

The words had streamed through my mind, and thus to God's, like water from a tap. I wished I could have retracted them even as I thought of them, realizing that I had betrayed Pete's confidence. Except that, just as I had heard God's lament, so apparently had every shade in heaven, so probably it didn't matter. I made another effort:

"What is the problem that caused you to be depressed, Lord? Was it because humans have behaved badly?"

I had great hopes for Earth. I have them no longer. I thought the human species could evolve to the degree that its members had freedom of will and powers of reason, and that reason, being such a magnificent faculty, would enable them to achieve a rational, just, and compassionate world society. I learned that reason can take them in the wrong direction just as readily as in the right one. My confidence had already been undermined by something else that has happened in the last few thousand eons. The universe is expanding at an accelerating rate, galaxies thrust apart from each other by dark energy, new galaxies failing to form, time in which wise and enlightened civilizations could emerge cut short.

"But didn't you set it up that way?"

I thought that by now advanced civilizations of intelligent beings would have begun to master comic forces.

"But, Lord, you could master the cosmic forces yourself!"

My purpose was to create creators.

"But it was a great thing having created heaven and allowing those who lived worthy lives—I mean fairly worthy lives—to enter it after they die! I think setting that up was a magnificent creation, Lord."

How long did you think I would keep processing trillions of arrivals from each of countless planets?

"Forgive me for asking, oh Lord, but what would you do if you didn't continue your present work?"

There are other universes.

"God, I mean gosh, I mean God, I've heard there might be multiple universes. So are you only in charge of this one?"

I let it get out of control.

"Still, it's still quite spectacular what you accomplished. If you'll forgive me for asking, may I ask how many other intelligent species on other planets evolved the way humans did on Earth?"

About one per every twelve hundred super galaxy clusters, but not a single one that has developed advanced technology has worked out, and that includes your own human species.

"Respectfully, permit me to ask: What do you mean that the human species didn't work out? We've had lots of evildoers and messed up the planet, but look what we've accomplished in technology, art, and so forth; even in good works. Isn't there a chance that humans will become more enlightened? They've learned a lot, after all, and in many respects behave better than they used to. Isn't there still a chance that they won't self-destruct?"

They are like every other advanced civilization in my universe, and, my Earthly fellow, it's got me down.

"Maybe we (I mean not you and me, God, but you and *humans)* can do it. If only you'd give a little help. Maybe it's time you started answering a few prayers."

Do you know what kind of prayers I get? Most of them like "Dear God, please make Malibu Mike win the sixth race at Santa Anita."

"I can see how that would be annoying, Lord, but I'm talking about high-quality prayers, like 'Please end this terrible drought, so the crops we have planted will come up and help prevent malnutrition of innocent young children."

Make it easy. Is that your idea? A universe where everything that happens is in response to high-quality prayers and no one has to think about anything or meet any challenges or overcome obstacles?

Despite my efforts to comfort him, God remained in the same melancholy, almost despairing, mood and stayed silent so long that I thought I wouldn't hear anything more, but he resumed:

I knew there would be hard times and suffering, and I felt badly about it, but if you're going to create an intelligent species you have to give them free will. I counted on the human capacity to calculate probabilities and analyze contingencies. I would watch the unfolding of a supremely rational and good society. From time to time there were indications that this might happen. But always, again and again, I witnessed greed, cruelty, and folly on every continent and in every culture, driving population increase ever closer toward the breaking point, ravaging forests, fouling aquifers and water courses, spewing plastics and toxins in the oceans, decimating fisheries. Where once fish of every color and variety swam, I see detritus swirling

about bleached reefs. Humans are a malignant variation of intelligent life in the process of annihilating
itself. You can't imagine how close I've come to getting it over with, destroying Earth.

God paused and I quickly interjected:

"I'm glad you haven't, Lord. If you had, many people who
are kind and loving and self-sacrificing would have been killed.
You would have been throwing out the baby with the bath
water, if I may draw upon a well-spoken proverb."

God was silent, and knowing that it would mean nothing for
him to spend the equivalent of a dozen or a dozen million Earth
years before communicating to me again, I tried to think of an
idea that would engage him. It came to me:

"Lord, have you read the book by Professor Stephen Pinker
titled *The Better Angels of Our Nature*. He carefully documents
how human societies are becoming less violent. Sure, there are
still plenty of horrors being perpetrated every day, but when
you consider that when I died there were seven billion people
and most of them were living ordinary peaceful lives and that
there had been no world wars in over half a century, it's evident
that people are learning to cooperate, that ongoing enlightenment and improved education has reduced the amount of
violence. So you see, there's plenty of reason to hope our species
will work things out and not descend into mindless anarchy."

Enough! Does Professor Pinker talk about the violence humans inflict on the oceans, aquifers, lakes, and
water courses, pumping ever increasing amounts of
toxic gases and particulates into the atmosphere, ruin-
ing wetlands, decimating marine life, driving global
warming, producing ever more destructive droughts,

fires, storms, floods, and rising sea levels, threatening to displace large populations from their homelands, which will bring about the premature deaths of billions in the coming decades? Does he mention that in the past few years two million people have been slain in the Sudan and a million more displaced and the figure grows every day. Does he write that humans have failed to act collectively for the good of their species and that their tenure on Earth will be for no longer than a tiny fraction of that of the dinosaurs? You can compile all the statistics and graphs you want, but the graphs don't show the suffering and cruelty or the number of people whose lives are stunted and who die prematurely of pollution and the exhaustion and poisoning of resources and will die in the future as population grows beyond sane limits and Earth's resources shrink and the whole planet increasingly stinks of air pollution, and its coastal regions yield to the rising seas. That there has been no war as all-encompassing as World War Two for the better part of a century is gratifying, but it's largely been a matter of luck. Sectarian strife continues unabated. Nuclear warfare would radically reverse all statistics and charts within minutes. Nuclear proliferation continues. I'm not omniscient as to the future, but I'm omniscient as to the present, and I take the long view, which humans have shown themselves incapable of doing, and I can tell you that your Professor Pinker is whistling in the dark.

Whew! There was no doubt in my mind that God's emotions had gotten the better of him. His latest rant removed any doubt in my mind that he was having a full-blown nervous breakdown. Indeed it seemed to me that he had become almost psychotic! Of course, knowing God was privy to these thoughts, I tried to suppress them, but I knew that the chance of succeeding in that was nil.

"Please God," I communed, "I can understand why you're discouraged, but as you said, you don't know the future. Maybe humans will pull it off. Maybe instead of destroying their planet, despite many setbacks and backslidings and tragedies, they will gradually become more enlightened and less selfish and foolish. Please give them a chance."

For someone who in his life was a greater knave and a fool than most, you've shown a speck of goodness.

Then the dark iridescent form before me vanished, God, not me, having moved, leaving me shaken and bewildered, but his remark about my showing a speck of goodness lifted my mood a smidgen above total hopelessness. Maybe I would be spared after all. Of course it mattered tremendously to me that God spare the world—I'd feel terrible if he destroyed it—but to tell the truth I was more concerned with my own fate. I didn't want to go to hell. It was as simple as that.

On I drifted through the unbounded reaches of heaven. I wasn't uncomfortable. I could feel the divine spirit that permeated this vast space. I felt grateful that I was still here and still had hope.

Yet (in heaven there always seems to be a "yet"), it was not long before I perceived heavy black clouds approaching. Closer they came, and closer still, until they dominated space in all directions, then enveloped me completely.

At once, I realized that they were clouds of despair, for they comprised my past selves, whose behavior I was once responsible for, but according to the shade of a renowned lawyer no longer am because they no longer exist. Despair, because, though they no longer exist, though there is no one self, each iteration of what I was exists forever in the spacetime landscape, each a minute fixture of the cosmos stretched out through past time.

"Peace, oh Earth-bound mind!" I cried: "Am I not in heaven?" If so, it was no profit to me: Spiritual bliss had dissolved in acrid memories; my heavenly state had become a pool of regret, and beyond regret, wistfulness, a more powerful emotion still, for

> . . . what we have we prize not to the worth
> Whiles we enjoy it, but being lack'd and lost,
> Why, then we rack the value; then we find
> The virtue that possession would not show us
> While it was ours.

"Let us not burden our remembrance with a heaviness that's gone." Prospero. But, having been, remembrance never can be gone. Heaven—eternal bliss—is incompatible with memories of a mislived life, for if memories are stripped away, who then would it be in heaven that you would call yourself, this memoryless bliss-experiencing entity that is the you you now are? Though incorporeal, I was still my earthly self, and all the powers of heaven could not change it.

16

These soul-consuming clouds passed, leaving me stunned and shaken, but once again surrounded by a limitless expanse of delicate blue.

A cloudlet approached at high speed, and I could see that it would pass close to me. Astonishments pile upon astonishments. Perched on it was my grandson Alex. It seemed to be he. At least this young fellow reminded me of him, except Alex was twelve years old and in good health when I died, which I thought was just a few days ago, and this was the shade of a man in his early twenties.

"Grandfather, he called. I was hoping to find you here. I'm happy you made it."

"You *are* Alex," I said, floating closer to him. "It's wonderful to see you, but saddens me you died while still a young man."

"Peace be with you," Alex called, already drifting on.

I was shocked to think that he was already dead. His shade appeared to be that of someone about ten years older than Alex as I remembered him. What happened in those ten years, *to* those years? It was a question I should have learned not to ask: passage of time is meaningless in heaven.

Though encountering Alex—Alex who had died so young—disturbed me, for a brief moment the experience freed me from the grip of despair, gave me a little thrill; but my mood darkened as quickly as it had brightened, the overpowering black cloud returning. I needed a miracle to fend it off, a thought that carried with it a rueful laugh: Heaven itself is a miracle!

Not enough of one.

And yet heaven is the one place, the only place, I believe, where a miracle can really happen, and one happened at that moment; transporting me from the hell of despair to the heaven of bliss.

Juliet had returned.

Once again I beheld her incomparable ethereal form. I contemplated her. I loved her anew. No Earthly substances do we need: "Drink to me only with thine eyes." Heaven has no greater bounds than those comprising Juliet and me.

She made a gesture that made me think of when I was a child in the hospital and a nurse brushed her hand across my forehead. Her touch conveyed the whole of love.

Why do my thoughts journey down these maudlin byways? Even when I'm with incomparably lovely Juliet!

"You are distraught, dear Jack," she said. "Then we are together, for I am too."

"You are an angel, as beautiful a creation as God ever fashioned, my Juliet. How could you be distraught?"

"God's malaise has worsened since we were last together. Heaven will not hold. The Lord is beside himself with woe."

"I know. I heard him again. He's thinking of destroying the world."

"And heaven too!" cried my angel.

"Juliet, my darling. Does God really have reason for such despair?"

"I am afraid he does, dear Jack. I have heard his laments, and know too that there has been even more on his mind than that to which he has confessed. What had been a magnificent and beautiful creation has turned into a universe-wide tragedy. Everywhere, civilizations rose, civilizations fell. The same sad process played out with each. Alas, dear Jack, I cannot tell you more. I love you more than you can know, but I love you in the service of God."

That last line threw me. I hadn't expected this sublime being to be cryptic with me. But here she was, rivaling Pete, Jesus, and God in that respect. I felt hurt, but then I gazed upon her, and I realized that I could not expect more from her than she was giving. I had been thinking of her the way I would on Earth if I had been keeping intimate company with a beautiful, brilliant woman of highest moral character and things weren't working out between us. But this wasn't Earth, and Juliet, though she deserved every accolade I could think of, wasn't a living breathing person; she was a true angel possessing the highest virtual physical and real spiritual graces. *Of course* she was in the service of God.

"That's all right, Juliet," I communed in a weak voice, and she continued:

"I can tell you that heaven is more chaotic than ever, dear Jack. It is a sad story. But be assured: Heaven will again be a place of spiritual perfection."

I was stunned, partly, I realized, because—and in honesty I should have admitted this earlier—the prospect of God's recovering from his illness terrified me. My judgment would no longer be delayed. Belatedly, truth shone blindingly in my mind: An atheist like me, and not the best kind, who had been admitted to heaven provisionally at most, would never gain permanent residency any place but in hell. Yet, even in the face of this, because I was in the presence of my incomparable Juliet, I felt a strange form of equanimity engendered by her love and compassion, which I felt radiating from her like warm rays of the sun on a bitter cold day.

"Thanks for telling me these things, dearest Juliet," I said. "Are you permitted to say whether there is anything I can do to stay in heaven?"

"My advice, dear Jack, is the same it would be if you were still on Earth. Be loving. Be strong."

Juliet was gone, and once again I was drifting through the cosmos, or through heaven, I couldn't be sure which. After all this turmoil, all these violent swings between hope and despair, I dwelled yet again on how my damnation must be certain. Even so, I resolved to follow the precepts Juliet had given me, and that resolution raised my spirits, so much did I love her, and I resolved to express that love the only way I could, by being faithful to her counsel.

Floating on through this nether region of heaven, I encountered a presence seated cross-legged on his cloudlet. He was absolutely motionless and conveyed no information, but in correspondence with some inner reference in my mind that I was unaware of, I knew it to be the shade of Siddhartha Gautama, the Buddha.

I had already found that heaven (once I was obliged to admit that it existed) was more capacious and its inhabitants more varied than I had imagined, and here was yet another individual, though he would deny that he was an individual, because he denied the idea of a self, who had no credentials in the theology postulating such a place.

In the time I was with the Buddha (if I can call it that, for as always in this realm, I had no sense of the duration of any experience), I felt myself changing in mood, attitude, and even philosophy, as if some powerful drug had suffused my being, this without a single identifiable thought passing from the Buddha's mind to my own.

How can he be in heaven? I wondered. Is this not a realm restricted to believers in Western gods? Is not heaven like an "exclusive" country club? That was a thought, I realized, that smacked of blasphemy. Since God was privy to my thoughts, I could be damned for thinking such a thing. What could be more exalted than heaven? And what could be more smarmy than an "exclusive" country club?

I said to the Buddha, "I am amazed to learn you could be here."

He turned to look at me.

"Heaven is designed to amaze," he said.

I started to address this revered personage as "your holiness," but checked myself since I assumed that heaven was run by the same God who according to the Bible said, "Thou shall have no other gods before me." Only then for the first time (including when I was still alive) did it occur to me that this First, or is it the Second, Commandment permitted people to have *other* gods, just none "before me." Literally construed, God's pro- hibition allowed other gods of equal stature to himself, and without limit! So, the system was looser than I'd always thought, and it would be acceptable to consider Buddha as another god, though I didn't think of him that way, but more like an exceptionally distinguished guru.

"Buddha," I communed, "I have always thought of you as being one of the wisest men who ever lived. When I was living

I had great respect for the Dalai Lama, who it seems to me more than anyone during my lifetime exemplified and personified your great teaching, as far as I know, for I confess that I'm quite ignorant of how your life and teachings relate to modern strains of Buddhism, of which I think Tibetan and Zen are the two main ones—"

I stopped in mid-sentence, feeling the force of the Buddha's disapproval, though not in the sense of a specific thought that he communed or even in his facial expression. It was more a matter of sensing a disharmony in the aether permeating space between us. And I became sure I was right in this when I received his next thought:

"As long as you are caught up in the illusion of self, you will always struggle and worry, but if you break free of your self, you will be in heaven, if there is a heaven."

"If there is a heaven? But isn't that where we are?"

"That is the question for you to answer."

The Buddha, having joined the ranks of Pete, God, Jesus, and even my beloved angel Juliet as an utterer of cryptic statements, resumed his pose, eyes directed ahead as if contemplating some universal truth, which though I might seek it forever I would never find. I closed my eyes and made a low humming sound, what I imagined was the tone corresponding to the frequency of the microwave background radiation that suffuses all physical space. I thought of how I was not a *self*, that I was a minute speck in the unimaginably vast cosmos, the ever roiling, silent cosmos, a limitless sea unruffled by wind and tide. Endless nothingness, formless.

Perhaps it was because of the influence of the Buddha that instead slipping into a dreamless sleep (and, by some earthly measure of time, centuries might have passed before my next thought came to mind), I felt nothing.

When my self-awareness returned and I opened my eyes, the Buddha was still seated before me, and this process repeated more times that I can remember, and each time when I once again became self-aware, the Buddha was still seated before me, and I thought of the phrase "eternal recurrence" (Nietzsche's, I think), and his presence reassured me and gave me peace, but then a timeless period passed, after which the Buddha was gone, and in this instance my *self* had returned and with it all my anxieties. I may have reached Nirvana, but had fallen back, as if recycled, ready for a replay of my ordeal, though it occurred to me that I might no longer be the same self as before.

I had no time to think about this further, for now there were others in my company, a great number of shades, each seemingly alone within the crowd they constituted. I wondered if they were new arrivals, waiting to be judged. I watched them, male, female, some old, some young, of all ethnic derivations though mostly oriental, perhaps reflecting the great proportion of the human population that is East Asian.

There is something about heaven, something like a force of physics inapplicable to the realm of the living, that drew me toward shades who when I encountered them I would find to be familiar, or of unusual interest. I assume that this force must work that way for all other shades as well, generating for each an endless succession of fortuitous encounters. That phenomenon may contribute to the joy one supposedly feels in the heavenly realm. Can it be that heaven is like some vast social network where friends and family members are linked without knowing it, but are drawn together through forces analogous to those that govern the behavior and movement of particles in the physical world and cause their world lines—their trajectories through spacetime—to congregate?

Shades retain linkages formed when they were earthly beings, so from the perspective of each shade—from my perspective, for example—someone with whom I was linked during my lifetime may emerge from among the millions, even billions, of others regardless of where they were in the measureless bounds of heaven and be in my presence for a while, then just as suddenly disappear. Where they go I know not, just as I know not where I go when I recede from the company of other shades.

This phenomenon played out now as I recognized a lightly bearded elderly gentleman, my mother's father, not my grandfather Thomas but my grandfather Robert, who died a few years later. I saw him only the two times in my life when he visited our family from his home in Chicago. He was a widower, and I remembered him as a slightly hunched man of average height, a dignified old gentleman, you might have thought if you had seen him.

"Grandpa," I called. He looked at me oddly. Of course he had only known me as a boy, but for some reason I had imagined that he would recognize me.

I thought with a cold heart (as if I were still alive and had a heart!), of how I could remember only one thing grandpa Robert ever said to me, and that was when I was four or five years old.

He said, "Sit on my knee and I'll tell you a story."

I complied and waited for him to begin. He smiled and chanted:

I'll tell you a story about Johnny McGrory,
And now my story's begun.
I'll tell you another about John and his brother,
And now my story is done.

He let me down from his knee, and let me down from my high spirits.

But my mother revered him, and he was a generous and gentle man. So I was willing to believe. Without even thinking about the virtue of forgiveness, I gave him a friendly wave.

He looked at me blankly, still not seeming to recognize me. Finally, he gave a perfunctory nod. I felt it showed that he knew we were connected, or might be connected. I tried to sense his thoughts, but sensed nothing. I had a strong feeling that nothing resided inside his head, under that shaggy white mane. On Earth, he couldn't rise above telling me a non-story, ignoring me while pretending not to. In heaven he seemed unable to communicate at all.

Then it occurred to me that I had recognized him at once because he resembled the self he was at the time he died, age seventy-seven, but in *his* memory I must still have been a child. How would I expect him to see that child in the shade of the man I was when I died?

Old grandpa Robert—I had seen him as if his whole life consisted of telling me that Johnny McGrory story when there was vastly more to his history than that, and he must have been a fine person or he would never have been allowed to stay so long in heaven. Perhaps he regretted having played that trick on me. It could have plagued him. I hope not. I hope he had merely misjudged how hurtful it had been to me. If he forgot it, fine with me. I'd like to think that his life was happy and not filled with regret; yet maybe it was because of that regret, that enlightenment, that he earned admittance to heaven. In all probability I would never know, for while I was thinking these thoughts he faded away, leaving me in a rueful mood, thinking of how I must have disappointed others the way he had disappointed me.

17

I had drifted far from my mooring, as I thought of that undefined and unrecognizable area where I imagined I had first met Pete, and reached an area of thicker, darker clouds among which flames flared as if from an unseen fire freshly stoked with fuel. I entered a region of turbulence, then some force displaced me and deposited me in an acrid area so suffused with a yellowish haze that on Earth it would doubtless have suffocated me or at least set off a pollution alert, but here, where breathing was not involved, merely put me in a state of discomfort.

It was then that occurred one of the most shocking events since I'd arrived in heaven. A glowering heavy-jowled male figure appeared before me. I recognized him at once. It was the shade of Richard Nixon!

No! I would have cried if I had possessed the means of vocalization rather than of silently transmitting thoughts, for my immediate reaction was that this was proof that I had been cast into hell. Only because that would have been too cruel a truth to bear did I deny its certainty.

"What are you doing here?" I demanded. "This is heaven. You shouldn't be here."

"The hell I shouldn't," he shot back. "I was maligned by the press, betrayed by colleagues. Then goddamn it, even though I made America great again, opened up China. Goddamn it . . . the way I was treated."

I looked away. My heart sank, again metaphorically, for I was a spirit and, although spirits are simulacra of human beings, they lack human organs. Not that a sinking heart is anything other than a metaphorical expression in the physical world! In any case, such proximity to Nixon made me feel closer to hell, if not already in it. The sight of him trampled into nothingness the last vestiges of any illusion that I might be admitted to heaven.

I turned back again. Nixon was gone, but other figures, even more sinister, floated by, ones with pasted-on smiles who made supplicating gestures, or threatening ones, like holding up the simulacrum of a fist as if about to bring it down on another shade's head. I saw no one else I recognized, but I could tell what sorts they were by their malevolent eyes. I wondered if that's the way I looked. I had failed in the most ordinary undemanding situations. At least I hadn't bombed Cambodia or breached my oath of office to uphold the law.

My next recollection was that I had left the region of sulfurous gloom and entered one where effulgent rays of light shone through backlit clouds. The shade of a woman was floating by. Her expression was beatific, raising my spirits. Surely she would not be in hell. And if she was in heaven, then, for the moment at least, so was I. Perhaps I had only *visited* hell!

"Stop," I called. "Can we commune? I am so confused. I don't know where I am. I just had an experience that made me feel I had wandered into hell. I'm happy I encountered you!"

She motioned with the simulacra of outstretched palms, trying to reassure me.

Meanwhile, I was thinking that she must be an angel. She

had no wings; yet her effect on me was no less miraculous. I felt myself growing calm—I was certain she would speak to me, and she did:

"Fear not, my friend. For heaven and hell are all the same. And the one in which you find yourself depends not on where you travel but on what you think and feel."

"I feel like I'm in heaven, talking to you," I said.

"Then you are."

On Earth, by now in such circumstances I would have felt romantic impulses, but in heaven spiritual bliss usually replaces amorous stirrings known to those still living, and so it did here.

"May I ask who you are?"

"Call me Cordelia," she said.

"*Call me?* Is Cordelia your real name?"

"It is whom I was called by Mr. Shakespeare."

"You were a contemporary of his? Amazing."

"I guess you could say so. He created me."

"Not Cordelia in *King Lear?*"

"I am."

"Fictional? I can't believe it. A fictional person can't become a shade in heaven!"

"With God all things are possible."

"Yes, so I've heard, but this is too much. I feel I'm going mad!"

I felt a caress on my shoulder, though it didn't seem she had moved, and I had no corporeal shoulder.

"I know something about men going mad," she said, "and you are not, but you don't understand the ways of God."

"I don't think God does either. I have heard his laments— you probably did too. Apparently he is seriously disturbed."

"Are you sure it was God you heard speak?"

"Why, of course. Who else would it have been?"

"Let me answer by quoting a friend of mine, a shade whose presence here might also surprise you—my brother, in a sense. Considering the same question in different circumstances, he said, 'the devil hath power to assume a pleasing shape; yea, and perhaps out of your weakness and your melancholy, as he is very potent with such spirits, abuses you to damn you.'"

"That sounds familiar. I could not have made the point as well."

"Nor could anyone else."

"Cordelia, I so admired you, and still do. Have you any advice for me."

"Honesty and courage, friend. Always." And like every other shade I had encountered in heaven, she vanished, leaving me wondering why those words about the devil were familiar. Could I have heard them from an angel guiding me when I was alive? They rang true. Pretending to be God is just the sort of trick the devil might try.

This explains everything, I thought. God lamenting, which seemed so unlikely, *not* the sort of thing God would do, was in fact a trick perpetrated by the devil! How could I for a moment have thought it was God who was saying that he was depressed? Yet, odd as that would be, or was, it would be no less odd if the devil had power to commit such a crime, broadcasting all over heaven! Still, it seemed possible. I trembled at the thought.

My speculations had taken me nowhere. All I could think of was that I was alone in what I had thought was heaven, but instead might be hell or some region unimagined by human beings, perhaps one of infinite chaos. I struggled to make sense of it.

I had no doubt that Nixon would be in hell and that Cordelia, if she had ever lived, would be in heaven. I had met them both in the same general region, except that in one area lay dark brooding clouds streaked with fire-stoked flames. In another effulgent rays of light shone through backlit clouds, producing natural beauty surpassing anything I'd seen on Earth. In proximity to these vistas the terror of hell washed over me. Could it be that heaven and hell were married? That they mirrored life on Earth?

Rintrah roars & shakes his fires in the burden'd air;
Hungry clouds swag on the deep.

Once meek, and in a perilous path,
The just man kept his course along
The vale of death.
Roses are planted where thorns grow.
And on the barren heath
Sing the honey bees.

Then the perilous path was planted:
And a river, and a spring
On every cliff and tomb;
And on the bleached bones
Red clay brought forth.

Till the villain left the paths of ease,
To walk in perilous paths, and drive
The just man into barren climes.

Now the sneaking serpent walks
In mild humility.
And the just man rages in the wilds
Where lions roam.

Rintrah roars & shakes his fires in the burden'd air;
Hungry clouds swag on the deep.

— WILLIAM BLAKE

18

What I then experienced was too intense for me to assimilate, and I lapsed into a state of unawareness that, as far as I can remember, ended only when I found myself once again on a rug-size cloudlet in a sea of them extending as far as I could tell above, around, and below me in space permeated by that delicate shade of blue I associated with the benign region of heaven I first beheld after my ascent.

Who was this shade drifting closer? It was someone I knew or someone I never knew but recognized because during his life he was a celebrity. I watched him closely. He was approaching the shade of a woman of dark complexion. They entered into conversation. He communed something emphatically. I perceived that they were exchanging thoughts, but couldn't make out what they were. What was it they were talking about? They smiled and laughed. He gave a little bow and moved on.

I floated closer to him.

"Hello," he called in a friendly tone. He was not young, but trim, and looked as alive as one could in this realm where all are dead. Heaven restores youth to a considerable degree. No one has trouble moving; shades are lithe. That alone is something to appreciate.

"Hello," I returned the greeting. "You look familiar."

"Maybe you've seen my picture," he communed. "I don't think we've met. You're an interesting-looking fellow. I think I would have remembered you, but I'm glad to meet you for the first time."

"Jack Treadwell's my name," I said. "Or at least it was before I died."

"Then it still is!" said my new friend. "Might as well hang on to what we can."

"Good point," I said; "and what's your name sir?"

"Studs Terkel."

"Really. Wonderful. I read a couple of your books. You were a national treasure!"

"Somewhat tarnished and needing polishing, especially near the end, but thank you."

"Well, Studs. I'm honored to meet you. How was it for you? Your death and getting into heaven? And *staying* here!"

"It's been touch and go, believe me. But that's the way my whole life was, so I've been able to handle it pretty well. How long have you been here?"

"Just arrived . . . a few days, weeks, years. . . . In heaven, who can say?"

"Nobody. No way of telling how long it's been between any two events. Time is the screwiest thing here, but there are some others close behind it."

"Do you think we'll get to stay? Have you been judged?"

"That's what I've been asking everybody," Studs communed. "There's a lot of misunderstanding about how heaven works. I never believed in it when I was alive, and still have my doubts even though I'm here. I don't know what's going on, but I do have a theory. One thing for sure: this place is in crisis, and the problem goes right up to the top."

"To God."

"That's the top as far as I know."

"I heard his lament, in fact two of them, if it really *was* God's voice I heard in my mind. Someone I met, shade of an honest woman, I'm sure, said that it may have been the devil."

"Don't think so. God runs the show here."

"Yeah, I'm sure this shade is honest and wise, but I happen to know that she has a limited frame of reference. At this point it seems totally unpredictable what will happen."

"That's a fair statement."

"So what should we do? How do we keep from being cast into hell? I worry about it. I can hardly think of anything else."

"Wish I knew," Studs communed, "but as I said, I do have a theory, and I've been getting some confirmation of it. Have you been thinking more about your bad behavior in life?"

"As a matter of fact, yes."

"Feeling worse about it since you got here?"

"That's right. Obsessing about how it must have felt to the people I wronged."

"Any women, by chance."

"How did you guess?"

"It was a good guess because you're a man."

"Pretty common, I imagine."

"Talk to enough people you get a feel for what goes on in human societies. The more I see of them the more they look alike. I lost my wife. She died—much too early. And I lived too long. Maybe that's why I think about things more than most people. But talk to almost any shade. How you feel about your life comes down to whether you made other people feel better or worse. That's what most of morality is about."

"Well, Studs, it's true I've been thinking a lot about the ways

I treated people badly or didn't treat them decently when I could have. And thinking about how it hurt not only them but me too, and it's been plaguing me. I can't stop thinking about it."

"Same for nearly everybody I've talked to," Studs communed. "That's what's given me an idea as to what's going on. And since I first thought of it, I've practically found proof of it."

"What's the theory?"

"That there's no special geographical place that's heaven and neither is there one that's hell. Heaven and hell are in *you*. And I suppose purgatory too. So to the extent you're feeling all this remorse, feeling rotten, then you're in hell."

"I've heard something to that effect from others, and felt it myself. It's a plausible theory," I said. "But I saw the shade of Richard Nixon. He's been here a long time and he showed no signs of remorse, though he certainly wasn't in a state of bliss, cussing, complaining. He seemed no different than I would have expected if I'd met him on Earth. In fact, I thought, if he's here, it can't be heaven. Then I thought—maybe he tricked his way in."

"He may well have," said Studs. "In any case, he's such a stubborn character—remorse hasn't taken hold of him yet. From what I've seen, it will. It will suddenly come over him, and he'll turn into a completely different kind of shade, but not a happy one I'm afraid. You see the heart of my theory is that in heaven, often quite quickly—but for some thick-skulled guys like Nixon it may take a lot longer—you become enlightened. That is, you gain a full appreciation of what sort of behavior is noble and good and kind and what is mean, manipulative, dishonest, and rotten. Against this new standard you look back on your life in a way that you never could when you were alive:

you see precisely and accurately how you measured up. So there's no punishment administered by God. Your punishment is clear-eyed enlightened contemplation of whatever gap there was between how you should have behaved and how you did behave. And if that gap is very large, the punishment can be very painful indeed!"

"It's an impressive theory Studs, and you may be right. Still, Nixon didn't show any signs of enlightenment when I saw him, and he's been here a long time."

"Remember, long time isn't a meaningful concept here. I've found that from interviewing hundreds of shades of all types. And I've found as to remorse and suffering, with most shades who have lived decent lives it's pretty mild, and most of the time it sets in as soon as shades get here, or even before; in fact quite often when they are still alive but approaching death. Others don't feel a twinge of remorse even in their dying breath—and from what you say that's the way it is with Nixon. It takes a while, even what on Earth would be decades, but, with a guy like that, at some point he'll still be in heaven, but it won't be heaven in his mind, which is what counts."

"*Mind* is a funny concept here. I associate it with living people."

"That's natural. But we have minds here too. In fact that's *all* we have."

"I like your theory, Studs, but why is it that Pete spent a lot of time threatening to send me to hell—he even put me on trial. I got the feeling I'd be there now if it hadn't been for God's being depressed, which delayed judging procedures."

"Pete warned me that I might be sent to hell too. As far as I can tell, he warns and threatens every shade who arrives here. He basically goes through a big act, the point of which is to stimulate new shades to become enlightened, to see their lives as they really were rather than how they fooled themselves into thinking they were."

"Studs, I'm pretty sure you're right. In fact I think it's working with me. I've been seeing my life in an increasingly bright light, and feeling all the anguish that it produces. So, the next question I have is: Does this become permanent? Is this the way it will always be for us? If we see our lives in the true light, will we come to terms with it and eventually feel blissful or will we always be filled with anguish over how we acted and how we *should* have acted?"

"Can't be sure. It may depend on factors we're not aware of. Tell me this, Jack. What would make you feel that you'd really made it to heaven?"

It was a question that caught me off guard. I wanted something—a heavenly experience—and didn't have any idea what it was. But then I did, and it surprised me: "Variety," I said. "That's what I need. Sameness for eternity would be horrible, even if it's blissful sameness. It scares me almost as much as the prospect of hell."

There followed, I think followed, but might have preceded, or neither followed nor preceded, one of those lacunae, a period I might liken to unconsciousness, dreamless sleep. But, since one does not sleep in heaven, and I'm not even sure one can be unconscious in heaven, it may be that events occurred in which I was a participant, but have no memory of them. I do remember that my day ("day" being short for non-discernible period, "period" necessarily being a metaphor of a unit of time, just as "time" is a metaphor for apparent non-simultaneity of events), was brightened by Stud's returning. I could sense that he was happy about something.

"Any news?" I communed.

"I think so," he replied. "I've had strong confirmation of my theory that heaven and hell aren't separate regions in the after-life, but are in your own soul or mind or whatever. I'd hardly left you when I encountered Nixon, and he was quite changed from the way he was when you saw him."

"How so?"

"He was standing on a cloudlet, and though, like all of us, he was incorporeal, he was twisting about, going into all kinds of contortions, struggling to keep his balance, first on one leg and then on the other, all the while trying to kick himself!"

"Mad at himself."

"Exactly—trying to kick himself around, which was what he complained others were doing to him."

"I wonder what's going on in his mind."

"I think it's the agony of enlightenment about himself. In time he may come to terms with it. But forget about Nixon. I have another case to show you, and this one is even more dramatic. Much more! Come with me."

I floated along, following Studs, happy to be on an adventure and getting a better idea of how heaven works. In due course we entered a region peppered with dark and ominous clouds, which thickened as we continued on. I wondered if there would be enough light to see anything, but gradually I could see better, as if my eyes were getting used to low illumination the way they did when I was alive.

I heard the sound first—one of the few I had heard in heaven. Someone was moaning and sobbing uncontrollably. Then I saw the hunched-over shade of a man, his hands sometimes covering his face, then his whole incorporeal form flailing, hopelessly, mindlessly, senselessly.

"Move over here, so you can see his face, though it's pretty horrible to look at," Studs said.

I followed Stud's instructions and didn't see much at first, because this shade kept his face mostly covered up. Then, flailing his arms, he turned his head toward me. His expression was horribly contorted, skin sagging. He scratched violently at his face, and with horror I realized that he had scratched out his eyes, then that he had ripped off his ears. He would have been unrecognizable were it not for the only part of his face that was not horribly disfigured, a clipped, dark, bristly patch of mustache that I recognized at once: all that was left of Adolf Hitler!

The contorted figure hunched over, covering his face with his hands, and rocked, heaving great sobs accompanied by harsh noises, like those of whooping cough patients gasping for air.

"My God it can't be, here in heaven!" I cried.

"It is," Studs communed. "He ripped out his eyes trying to banish the sight of his millions of victims and ripped off his ears in hopes of silencing their screams, but he can't banish the sight or sound of them from his mind, or soul, or whatever you want to call it. Heaven may be around him, but there's no heaven in his head, or mind. He's in the hell of understanding what his life was about."

"Still, I'm surprised that God didn't cast him into the flames of hell," I said.

"An angel I interviewed told me that once Hitler realized how evil he'd been, he prayed for just that, and God turned him down."

"I wonder if he was being clever, thinking that anything he wanted would be turned down and that he might protect himself against being sent to hell by saying it's what he wanted!"

"Not possible. God would have read his mind. No, he is *that* miserable. Because he got enlightened, he's nothing now but a steaming cauldron of remorse. Utter anguish. Beyond what we can imagine. That is his essence, the totality of Hitler's shade."

Studs and I drifted on, and I was still reeling from having witnessed the torture remorse can impose on a shade at its full extreme. I thought about how everything you've done in life is permanent. Nothing is erased. Studs and I talked some more, and I came to agree with him that what happens when you get to heaven is not eternal bliss, though that still may be a possibility. What you get, no matter how you acted in life, is enlightenment—a true and full understanding of to what extent your life was marked by compassion, kindness, and mindfulness and to what extent by selfishness, cruelty, and mindlessness. For some, as in the case of the supremely evil wretch we had just observed, that understanding is the equivalent of the innermost circles of hell.

Though I accepted Studs's theory intellectually, it bothered me emotionally. "I still can't believe it," I said. "Hitler tortured by his enlightenment. You could almost feel sorry him."

"Well, actually, no," said Studs.

"If I'd been God, I would have pitched him to the flames," I said.

"Showing compassion," Studs observed.

"How long do you think this will keep up? Are we talking about experiencing remorse *forever?*"

"I don't have a handle on it," Studs communed. "Like anything to do with time here, the concept of 'forever' doesn't make sense."

We continued on a while in silence, our faithful cloudlets moving with us underfoot.

"What I have yet to find out," Studs communed, "is whether

people, shades, whatever you want to call them, have *fun* here in heaven. There should be some payoff for people who behaved all right in life or came fully to terms with how badly they acted, and to my mind that should be not eternal bliss so much as *fun*!"

"You're exactly right," I said. "Maybe it's been arranged for really good people, but we weren't good enough to merit it. We're not utterly miserable like Nixon, much less Hitler, but we're not having that good a time. Well, count your blessings, I suppose, as my grandmother used to say. I'm amazed that I'm here at all."

"Same here," Studs communed. "When I figured out where I was, I thought there must have been a slip-up at the admissions desk: then I decided that God is more tolerant than I'd given him credit for."

Studs's shade was beginning to drift away. I knew he'd be gone in a few moments. It always seemed to work that way: people drifted into your presence, or you into theirs, but you couldn't hold onto them. It happens in life too. Not to lapse into melancholy again. I had no cause for it. Talking to Studs had made me feel better. I wasn't quite feeling happy, but I felt that maybe there was hope for me after all.

Next thing I knew—I had been unconscious—I became aware that I was lying on my back in my bed in the hospice, feeling slightly nauseated, head elevated, my eyes closed and not wanting to open them because of the brightness coming though my eyelids, something pressing against the inside of my arm, and something else against my nose, an awareness that I was catching my breath, something that never happened in heaven, and almost thinking that I was back on Earth; the pressure of a hand on my arm. I let my eyelids peel back and looked up at a low sky, which I quickly realized was in fact the ceiling.

"You surprised us, Mr. Treadwell," said a voice, which I recognized as that of Dr. Kapp. "The new drug we've been treating you with has been an astonishing success. Just as important, and necessary, you were successful in withstanding the stress of it. You have a remarkable constitution. I'll be writing a paper on this for the *American Journal of Neurology*. You can bet they'll accept it. This is an extraordinary case, and I have to say that I didn't think I could achieve the result I did— that you would ever open your eyes. You can't imagine what's involved medically speaking."

I said nothing. I felt exceedingly tired. I might be capable of talking and even sitting up in bed, but I closed my eyes again and lay still. If I exhibited further amazing neurological results, who knows what outpouring it would have brought forth.

I heard a murmuring of voices, then nothing; then I sensed that less light was penetrating my eyelids. Lights in my room had gone out, and there was only the still considerable light from the hallway in which nurses must be striding back and forth, outpacing visitors solemnly walking toward the rooms in which their loved ones lay ever closer to death or retreating through the glass-paneled door leading to the reception room, nodding and smiling weakly at the receptionist and passing through the revolving door into the province of the not yet dying, relieved to be glancing up at the leafed-out trees and the street lamps spreading their light on the sidewalks and pavement.

Then I was asleep, or so it seemed, and perhaps dreaming, or perhaps dozing. In any event a considerable interval of time may have elapsed, the duration of which I never became aware before I walked out of the hospice to the amazement of the staff and my niece, Emily, who had come to take me home and arranged for a practical nurse to attend to me for as long as it would take, a period when I could read and write and see friends and listen to music (all sacred music). But, if this occurred, the specifics of it are lost to my memory; indeed, it may have only happened speculatively, for what I do remember, and in perfect detail—there was no doubt this time—I was walking along a path in a dense and darkening wood, which was becoming better defined as it descended. Ahead it was marked by a sign that said, "Abandon every hope, who enter here."

I screamed without making a sound, shaken, wakened from my second dream since I'd gone to heaven, one even more unsettling the first.

19

Drifting alone through the soundless expanse of heaven, still shaky in the wake of this latest disorienting event, I tried to make sense of what had happened to me, and wondered if sense could be made. My most recent dream, with its terrifying end, seemed inexplicable and unresolvable. I was almost as afraid I might start dreaming again as of being sent to hell.

It was not another dream that supplanted every trace of my consciousness, but, again, this time without warning, the voice of God:

More and more I've been of a mind to destroy the Earth. There are plenty of asteroids available for such a purpose. Or I might choose a magnificent flare from the sun to do the job. Whoosh, singe, fry, leaving a few trillion trillion subterranean bacteria to make a fresh start. Fie! Such is the perniciousness of religion that there are always crackpots proclaiming that this is exactly what I'm about to do. What a glorious last few seconds they would have as the sky lights up with hot flares and lightning strikes every square meter of ground.

Ah, oh, there is wisdom in the well-spoken proverb,

"You made the bed, now you can sleep in it." I created
this mess. It would be too easy, too unworthy, simply
to scrub it away. Except, damn it. Damn it! It would
stop the suffering!

The voice in my mind ceased, but I was stunned as if by a
blow in the head. God sounded—what can I say?—dangerous!
I know not how long it would have been by any measure of
time before my brain began to stir again, analogs of neuronal
currents struggling to make meaningful connections. My
psyche, my very being, was shattered. When at last I managed
to piece together intelligible thoughts, only one course seemed
rational: I would follow Buddha's example and escape from
myself. Not deny myself, but deny my *self*. To this end I tried
to contemplate the great cycles and the chaos of life on Earth.
How odd it was, I thought, how surprising, that the same
conditions seemed to be obtain in heaven as well.

My attempt at mindful contemplation—a sort of fixed
attentiveness removed from *self*—enabled me to drift into a
meditative state. During the course of the following I don't
know how long a period anxieties invaded my reveries from
time to time, but I sensed that I was making progress, progress
in the sense of shedding any sense of progress! I might not find
eternal bliss in heaven, the sort fancied by optimistic Christian
theologians, but maybe I could reach Nirvana, which for all I
knew is the best to be had.

My transformation continued in this respect, and my eyes
had been closed for what I speculated might have been an
extended length of time, when I impulsively opened them and
beheld my darling Juliet.

So much for attaining sublime indifference! How beautiful she looked, and, as if knowing that my contemplating her would provide all the happiness I could wish for, she communed no thoughts, but remained suspended silently before me.

Your being here is enough for me, I thought. I have reached true heaven. This is what it must be, a state of being where everyone has a personal angel of such beauty and radiance that granting eternal contemplation of her (or him for those who prefer) is God's means of bestowing the gift of eternal happiness that humans have longed for since they first became self-aware.

After one of those what on Earth I would call lapses of time, Juliet communed: "Jack, dearest, you have noticed that heaven has changed, have you not?"

"Yes, and you must be referring to how God is depressed and distraught, which has thrown the heavenly realm into disarray."

"It may have started as depression, but since I saw you last, God's mental state has worsened. He has become so dispirited, I can hardly bear to say it . . ."

I wanted to comfort Juliet and embrace her, but she floated to a greater distance from me, I think to remind me that physical contact with an angel can never come to pass. She continued:

"What I say now is important for you to know, Jack. It is in the nature of the workings of the multiverse that God is being transferred. He will become God of another universe, a simpler one where higher life forms cannot evolve. It is a beautiful universe, but a sterile one. There God can spend tens of billions of years resting and regaining his equanimity."

"This is startling news indeed, my dearest. Won't our Lord get bored in such a place?"

"Not at all. He can keep himself busy fine tuning physical laws and observing the unfolding of cosmic processes without having to look upon living beings the character of whom he can not bear."

"This is so amazing, my darling Juliet. What does it mean for our universe, and for us?"

"A new God will take over our universe. What that means for us I cannot tell you. I don't know what form heaven will take, but I'm sure it will become orderly and rational again. Chaos will no longer reign."

"When will this happen?" I asked, forgetting for the moment that in heaven "when" has no meaning.

"You will see, Jack dearest. You will see."

She came closer, and although we were both incorporeal minds enshrouded in phantasmal human forms, I felt, not just the effect of recalling a physical experience when I'd been alive, but the physical sensation itself, as if she had kissed me with a fervor I had never experienced before and never expected to again. Yet even at the moment of extraordinary sensation she was gone, leading me to conclude that rapture can occur in heaven, but is even more rare and fleeting than on Earth.

I basked in the sensation of that kiss for what seemed to me to be a substantial portion of eternity. It took on a significance that dwarfed anything that ever happened to me. Only gradually did I begin thinking about the coming of New God. What would he or she be like? New God might cast me into hell without giving it a second thought. And this might be *real* hell. With real flames leaping up around, about, and under me, condemned to eternal suffering beyond anything I could imagine, though perhaps New God would show mercy on bereft shades like me and on the countless suffering people on Earth too. It was useless to speculate.

On I floated it seemed, mentally hugging my cloudlet the way a child might hug a stuffed animal. At some point I realized that I was not just floating but was being pulled toward a place of special meaning in heaven. How I knew this I do not know, but I was certain that I was being summoned before Pete, and that God had given him leave to judge me.

I had been on the verge of subscribing to Stud's theory that hell and heaven were one realm and that we would spend eternity existing neither in a base region perpetually immersed in flames nor in one permeated with spiritual bliss, but in a realm where we would reach a state of unlimited enlightenment. I had been half convinced by it, more than half convinced, but I had not been completely convinced. Now I had a strong intimation that, whatever hell might be, it was about to open its maw to receive me, and Pete was about to deliver me to it.

Someone once said—I think it was Samuel Johnson—that the prospect of being hanged the next morning concentrates the mind wonderfully. The prospect of being condemned for eternity in hell has an even greater effect. I had been summoned before Pete in the past. Each time the results had been inconclusive. This time it seemed certain that judgment would be rendered and swiftly carried out.

20

My intimation that Pete had summoned me proved correct. Suspended in space, without even a cloudlet placed as if to support him, he stood positioned vertically in relation to me, expressionless, like a judge who takes care not to betray his feeling lest he be suspected of partiality. I tried to appear impassive as well, determined not to show fear. Perhaps it was a baseless notion, but I worried that betraying fear might be taken as a sign of my guilt.

You are wrong, Jack Treadwell, Pete communed. Though by now I was an experienced shade, I had forgotten that he knew my thoughts. *I am not going to pass judgment on you. I summoned you to let you know that this is the last time you'll see me.*

"What? How come?" I asked, not wanting to betray what Juliet had told me.

God and I are moving to another universe. God is content with that prospect, but it's terribly hard on me. There are no sentient beings there, so there will be no one for me to judge, no one on whom to practice my wiles and tricks, no one to amuse me. The import of this is that, after spending two Earth millennia sentencing others, I myself have been sentenced to an eternity of nothingness, staring at particles ripped from their molecular arrangements by dark energy, flying apart before they can condense into stars, particles that I perceive are there but aren't visible, because there is nothing to illuminate them except unvarying monochromatic low frequency radiation. God's new universe will become immensely larger than his old universe—your universe—but only because it's expanding at an unimaginably high rate of acceleration. Our Lord, who oversaw this dynamic, magnificent, inexhaustibly interesting cosmos for almost fourteen billion Earth years, will henceforth rule over an incalculably vast expanse of barely more than nothingness. There you have it, Jack.

"Gosh," I communed back. "I'm really sorry about this, Pete. I hope it will work out for the best."

Of course I was a lot more interested in my fate than in Pete's, and I was delighted that it no longer mattered that he was aware of what selfish unempathetic thoughts I harbored. The hell with him, I thought, barely trying to suppress it. I've escaped whatever judgment he and God might have meted out for me. Now it only mattered what New God would do. Would it be for better or for worse than with the old one? That was the question.

An eternity of nothingness, Pete resumed. *I deserved better!*

"Yeah, it's tough," I said. "Sorry."

It's so unjust.

"I know, Pete. It's just rotten."

Instead of your being cast into hell, Jack, which I know you've feared and certainly deserved, it is I who am being cast into an empty duller-than-dull universe. It is I who have been judged rather than you. It's appalling. Simply appalling.

"My God, I'm really sorry, Pete," I said, deciding I'd better express more seemingly heart-felt empathy. "How could this be? How could you be treated this way? After all, you're a saint. You served God for two thousand years, and I'm sure you served him well. That ought to count for something!"

I think I have, Pete communed. *But who says the way it is is the way it should be. I have to accept it.*

"In any case, I'm truly sorry that you are being reassigned against your will. I had gotten to like you in a way, Pete, even though I've been afraid of you—afraid of how you might judge me, in fact *have* judged me."

Thanks for saying that, Jack. This has been terribly hard on me, but it's good for you that I won't be around any more, because after reviewing the trial, even though you were represented by a slick lawyer and taking in what you've just been thinking, and even though in a way I like you, Jack, and I would like to retract anything hurtful I've said to you—

"Thank you, Pete."

Don't thank me too soon. I was about to say that even though I've lost everything else, I can at least preserve my honesty: for that reason I can't retract my opinion that in all justice you should be sent to hell.

"Pete, that's so disappointing to hear. Even before I died, I regretted how I'd treated people badly and hadn't been more honest and compassionate and mindful. And I felt remorse even more acutely once I got to heaven. I never prostrated myself and cried 'I repent,' or anything dramatic, but I died a good person and I've become a better shade. Even though you say I'll be spared for the moment because you and God are being transferred, it still hurts deeply that you'd send me to hell."

There, you defended yourself better than your lawyer did.

"So, will you change your mind? I mean, would you if you were still the judge?"

No, Jack. The multiverse may be unjust, but I will be true to my principles.

"I just don't understand. Now, after all our conversations,

and you were kind enough even to take me on a tour of a region of heaven, why are you so harsh and unforgiving?"

If you must know, it's because of your treatment of Sue Marcello. The fact is, Jack, I've grown very fond of her myself. It's salt rubbed into my wounds that she will remain in the same spiritual realm as you while I'll be sent off to I don't know what to call it. Your remorse is the equivalent of a nick that draws a few drops of blood, but you plunged a knife into Sue's heart. In fact I ought to send you to hell right now. Maybe I still have power to do so!

"That hurts, and I truly am miserable about it, and you should know that my remorse is even greater after what you just said. And I can appreciate why you've fallen for Sue. I was such—"

Never mind. I know what you're going to think before you think it. We won't see each other again, Jack, unless destiny unfolding over hundreds of billions or trillions or more of what on Earth you'd call years brings us together in yet another universe. For the present you'll be subject to the authority of the new regime.

"Yes, of course. I understand that. Can you tell me anything about it? Who is replacing you? I assume there will be someone filling your job. Will I have a chance with whoever, whomever, it is? Will there be a new trial?"

As I was formulating this last question, I thought of the principle of double jeopardy; then realized it wouldn't apply, because this is like a mistrial, like where the judge dies in the middle of it. And of course, it wouldn't apply in heaven anyway, which doesn't recognize laws of earthly jurisdictions.

I know this much. New God doesn't like to delegate, so there will be no one filling my job. You'll have to deal with him (excuse me, her, not her exactly, but more her than him) directly. I can't answer your other questions.

I felt once again that earthly-mimicking chill in response to Pete's hostility, but I thanked him and said I appreciated his giving me what information he could.

A lacuna occurred of the sort that had become so familiar to me, then for the last time Pete communed:

Farewell, Jack Treadwell. You give the impression of being a decent fellow, but you should be in hell.

HE WAS GONE, and I was alone again, in a heaven of a universe that, as far as I knew, was between Gods to run it. Presumably, all the angels, saints, and I, and countless other shades would sense New God's presence soon. She might endorse the setup that Studs thought had been established by Old God. She might set up a heaven and hell and who knows what other regions in between, or, despite what Pete had said, she might appoint a saint like him to judge who shall be admitted and who shall not.

Even with her super, beyond super, beyond quantum mechanical computer capabilities, would New God want to handle the round-the-clock onslaught of new shades streaming in here from Earth and who knows how many other planets scattered over the cosmos? Might she have a completely new policy, one that humble ex-mortals like me could never imagine?

For the moment I was not in danger, but I felt more helpless than ever, helpless, alone, beleaguered, and trapped in my own private hell of recollection of all the transgressions that I had glossed over, suppressed, and tamped down into a few out-of-the-way analogs of neural clusters where they could never be retrieved except under deep hypnosis or by some God-agent like Pete who knows all and from whom I could hide nothing, even what I'd hidden from myself.

Having arrived at a point in my stay in heaven where my spirits had sunk to new depths, as sometimes happens on Earth and much more often in heaven (which is why heaven, despite not living up to its reputation, is still the best place to find yourself after you die), something unexpectedly and miraculously wonderful happened.

Those of you esteemed readers who have accompanied me through these trials can probably guess what it was: Juliet had returned.

Swooping in on me, she communed, as always, with incomparable brio, "Hello, my darling Jack."

"I'm so glad to see you, angel of my dreams," I communed back. "I just spoke with Pete. He told me that he will be accompanying God to a new universe. I hope you are not leaving too. Please tell me you'll stay."

"If I didn't stay, Jack, I wouldn't be a true angel."

"That makes me feel better than anything I've heard since I got here. Do you know whether God has left by now and whether New God has arrived, and what his policy, if that's the right word, will be? Excuse me, her policy. Pete said that New God isn't male, and, if not exactly female, at least more female than male. Will she instantly know everything that's going on in our universe?"

"Here is what I have learned, dear Jack. New God was most recently God of a very different kind of universe, one not much different from the one Old God is taking over. Now, just as Old God was, she will be God for countless trillions of intelligent beings on countless thousands of planets in our universe, and for each particular species of intelligent beings New God will be God, just as if she were God *only* for each. You can be sure that she will be observing humans and their shades just as attentively as if we were the only species in her charge, but I have no idea what her policy will be. We must wait and see and accept whatever in her wisdom she decrees."

"I guess she could send me to hell, or create a new one if the old one isn't satisfactory and send me there."

"And even me, dear Jack. For all we know even angels may be anathema to New God, though that seems unlikely. New God has had experience being God in at least one other universe with intelligent self-aware inhabitants and probably countless others for eternal periods beyond reckoning, so we can have reason to hope that she will be wise. And to be wise is to be compassionate, would you not agree, dear Jack? But we can't be sure. She may be possessed of wisdom beyond our understanding. Looking back on Old God, I feel that at bottom he was a softie. It was his inability to continue witnessing human folly and cruelty that led to his mental breakdown. New God may be more tough minded."

This was not in the line of comforting assurances I was hoping to receive from my sublime angel, and, perhaps as a self-protective measure, my mind then lay dormant. Best as I can remember, I didn't exhibit any agitation or distress for a very considerable period before I began to regain some composure. Fortunately, I was braced by the enormous compassion and love I fancied my darling angel felt for me, and this conviction was somewhat buttressed as she communed to me:

"You have been brave most of the time so far, dear Jack, and you must continue to be brave and be brave all of the time. Have faith. And know that, even when you are not in my presence, I am with you."

"Can we send thought messages to each other, my sweet?"

"Dear Jack," I think I heard in my mind, but she was gone.

. . .

AFTER WHAT ON Earth would have been a lengthy interlude, I wandered lonely as a cloud (again), most of all missing Juliet and wishing she would return, though through mere contemplation of her, coupled with the recollection that we Treadwells are made of sterner stuff, I felt my energy and hope returning and that I was ready as I ever could be for the next phase of my afterlife.

I was eager to find Jeff, Studs, and my nephew Wally and, now that Pete was gone and not keeping me from her, my wife Ellie, and of course my sister Karen, and see how they were all doing and let them know what I had learned. I should be able to find them, I thought, for in heaven distances are nothing, nor is time, though I had no idea whether the links that allow for improbable encounters were still working, or what I must do to make them work. I floated on, hoping that we would be brought together just by my thinking about them.

21

An amorphous shape formed before me. I sensed thoughts emanating from it. I had been in heaven long enough (a couple of days? a couple of centuries?) to think I knew this was no ordinary shade, saint, or angel. It was New God herself communing to me.

I should have been totally attentive, but my mind wandered, dwelling on how astonishing it was that this one individual God, even though she had just arrived in our universe, was capable of communing to or with every shade in the heavenly realm and every intelligent creature in the physical realm on every planet in every galaxy in the universe, apparently at the same time if she wanted; yet from the perspective of any individual an exclusive one-on-one event was occurring. The quantum computer analogy had been explained to me several times. I knew I would never understand it.

I snapped back to attention to the matter at hand, thinking: This is it! I'm about to meet New God! I'll learn what her policy is and what it means for me. Indeed, at that very moment I felt New God's thoughts permeating my mind. At first, they were devoid of informational content, perhaps because she was still getting used to communicating in a completely new universe every event throughout the history of which she'd been required to assimilate almost instantly after she arrived. In any case, eventually, without benefit of words or particular statements, there became instilled in me an awareness that New God had judged me and found that I had behaved badly enough in life to warrant sending me to hell, except that in my final years on Earth I had gained some understanding of how I had hurt others and been dishonest, lazy, and self-indulgent (and like most people displaying such traits harmed myself in the process), and that I would have done myself a great deal of good if I had been self-disciplined and thoughtful as to the feelings of others and been alert to the effect of my behavior on them; that happily I had felt remorse and greater empathy by the time I died, and even more since then, almost but not quite enough to earn entry into heaven, and so I would have to spend some time in purgatory, except it was New God's policy not to have such a thing as purgatory, nor did New God intend to create such a place or state, but in her view there was a perfectly good alternative, which is life on Earth, and therefore, my case being an extremely close one, and New God, if not infinitely merciful, at least having a decent sense of fairness and considerable tolerance, would send me back to Earth to live a while longer.

Incredible, I thought. What great, great good fortune! I wanted to thank New God and praise her and give thanks again and resolve that as soon as I got back to Earth I would make some heroic and dramatic gesture like sacrificing a car or light truck to show my gratitude. I wanted to consider what rules I should formulate to express my worshipful allegiance to her dictates and her divine being, and urge all living humans to follow and spread the Good News of New God's arrival.

Just as quickly as these impulses stirred in my mind, I was shocked by them, for they gave indication of replicating thousands of years of misguided religiosity and pious practices in human history, which had so dismayed Old God during his tenure, and then I wanted to thank New God for vouchsafing me that bit of enlightenment, but sensed that she would find it tedious to listen.

What in the end I communed to New God (not that she wasn't doubtless aware of my intervening mental processes on the way to reaching my settled thought) bore no relation to any of such things, for I boldly asked:

"Oh, New God, if I return to Earth and awaken as if I've come back from the dead, will it be deemed to be a miracle?"

A reply came forth in verbal form that I could hear as clearly as if spoken on Earth:

Time is not a dimension in heaven. To observers on Earth you will have been gone for a few minutes.

New God vanished from my presence. It took awhile to absorb what she had communed. Could I really return to the realm of the living? It seemed inconceivable. But I had no time to ponder the question, because through some mechanism the nature of which shall always be a mystery to me, I was in motion, in what direction or at what speed and for how long I had no way of knowing, but at some point I came upon a place in heaven that seemed familiar. Perhaps it was the arrangement of cloudlets above, around, and below and the particular hue of the delicate shade of blue permeating all space that informed me. Confirming this intimation, I heard an enchanting series of tones of a brass instrument just as I had when I first arrived in heaven, but what I heard now was quite different. This was not the sound of angel Gabriel blowing his horn. It was more varied, syncopated, flamboyant, exciting, sensuous, and more—

I felt out of place even thinking it—*earthy*, and then I beheld the author of it, no one I ever imagined would be made into an angel, but indeed clearly had been.

This newly appointed angel of New God had a very dark complexion, and I realized that, astonishing as it was, he could be no one else than a person I would have recognized instantly had we both still been alive.

I let my visual senses rest and listened to the music, celebrating, it seemed, the marriage of heaven and Earth. I was close enough now to watch this angelic performer hold his trumpet aside, then listened to that rich gravely voice I remembered, singing:

> . . . Just direct your feet
> to the sunny side of the street.

The music faded and so did my vision of this aetherial scene, and I realized that I had passed through the same gates of heaven through which I had entered, passed through blackness, the imperceivable divide between the heavenly and physical realms, whereupon I winced at the once familiar, but almost forgotten, feeling of having a dull headache. Slowly, I opened my eyes and realized that I was looking up from my bed in the Burnside Memorial Hospice. I turned toward the sound of a living human voice, perhaps that of a nurse, and heard her say:

"He was only in a coma! He's coming out of it!"

EPILOGUE

It was an "astonishing remission," Dr. Kapp told me a few days later, and the following week she said that I was making "astonishing progress." Now, almost four months have passed since my return from heaven. I didn't think any of my acquaintances here at Arcadia Retirement Estates would believe I was there, and I wasn't so naive as to try to convince them. I just told them I'd had some fantastic dreams or hallucinations and that sometimes I couldn't tell which was which.

I'm still unsteady on my feet and can't always come up with the right word (or memory) when I'm talking, but—and this is like a miracle of a heavenly order—I'm not just in rehab, but in training, doing stretches and each day paddling back and forth in the therapy pool, trying to do a bit more than the day before, but mainly I'm trying to be more mindful, more sensitive to the feelings of others, reflecting on my transgressions, trying to avoid mistakes of the past, keeping up with the news and the lives of friends and family, calling or sending emails to everyone who might be pleased that I'm thinking of them; also emailing newspaper editors and office-holders, checking news from around the world, looking for signs as to how New God is going to treat us, and of course writing these notes about my afterlife, typing two or three pages most days even when I'm not feeling well.

Old God learned that just because intelligent creatures with spectacular reasoning powers evolved on Earth that didn't stop them from acting irrationally and cruelly. Will New God continue to put up with this, or decide to intervene? I wish I could tell you. My guess is that the ways of New God will prove to be as inscrutable as those of Old God. One thing I can say, based on intimations I've gotten, I'm quite sure that New God won't look kindly on being deluged with self-seeking prayers, or worshipful ones for that matter, any more than Old God did. For that reason, even though I could think of dozens of prayers, I'll limit myself to one:

New God, I realize you're not going to revise the laws of physics, and that we'll have to keep putting up with earthquakes, droughts, floods, and the like, but how about tilting the scales a little so we aren't so likely to self-destruct and destroy our planet. Infuse into our DNA a dominant kindness gene and ratchet up our honesty, empathy, and mindfulness a notch; or send everyone to heaven for a short course such as I had and return them to Earth to put what they learn into practice.

I'd appreciate it if you would convey good wishes to my friends up there—you know who they are. Finally, and I don't mean to be importunate, but would you please consider getting Juliet a new set of wings?

Tired from composing and murmuring my prayer, I closed my eyes and slept, and while I was sleeping, I had a vision that Juliet had alighted beside my bed.

"My darling," I whispered. "I thought you were not allowed to visit Earth."

"That was Old God's rule, dear Jack," she said. "New God not only gave me permission to visit Earth; she sent me to give you a message."

"I'm in awe of that," I murmured, "Please tell me what it is."

"Just this, Jack: You've dwelled enough on your sins and failings. Meditate on your virtues and celebrate what was good and noble in your life. Heaven will smile upon you."

Juliet vanished, and I woke up with a start, thrilled for a half second before realizing that she had only visited in a dream.

In heaven, except for my two nightmares, I had felt sure that I was *not* dreaming; this time I knew that I had been. Contrary to the way Juliet appeared in heaven, in this most recent visit she had been indistinct, and the entire scene was colorless, vague and ill-defined.

Mere dream though it was, might it have been a portent of how New God would judge me? That was a nice thought, but I told myself I shouldn't draw conclusions from a dream; then that maybe I should.

I DON'T KNOW when Dr. Kapp realized that my recovery was not to last. The day after I dreamed that Juliet had visited me, I suffered a relapse. Then—I don't know how long it was afterward, only that I had woken up and noticed it was just getting light outside, or just getting dark—I dazedly looked up into Dr. Kapp's gray-blue eyes, and she took my hand.

"Jack, it's time to move to the hospice again," she said; "later this morning. I think you know—this time you won't be coming back."

I nodded and smiled. She squeezed my hand; then, just like

the beings I'd met in heaven, almost as soon as she had entered into my presence, she was gone.

I have to assume Dr. Kapp is right about my having little time to live, but right now I'm propped up with pillows, typing these notes, still very much alive, and

When I am dead, my dearest.
Sing no sad songs for me;
Plant thou no roses at my head,
Nor shady cypress-tree:
Be the green grass above me
With showers and dewdrops wet;
And if thou wilt, remember,
And if thou wilt, forget.

I shall not see the shadows,
I shall not feel the rain;
I shall not hear the nightingale
Sing on, as if in pain:
And dreaming through the twilight
That doth not rise nor set,
Haply I may remember
And haply may forget.

— Christina Georgina Rossetti

END NOTES

Quotations from Literary Works

152 "Rintrah roars and shakes his fires . . ." William Blake, *The Marriage of Heaven and Hell*

164 "Abandon every hope, who enter here . . ." Dante, *The Divine Comedy*, tr. Allen Mandelbaum; Canto III

181 "Just direct your feet . . ." (performed in heaven by Louis Armstrong): *On the Sunny Side of the Street* (1930), composed by Jimmy McHugh, lyrics by Dorothy Fields

Special thanks to Ken Crawford
for permission to use his astrophotograph of
the Orion Nebula, M42, as a cover illustration.

About the Author

EDWARD PACKARD WAS born in 1931 in Huntington, New York and is a graduate of Princeton University and Columbia Law School. He conceived of the idea and wrote the first book and dozens of others for Bantam's classic Choose Your Own Adventure series, and wrote many other books for young readers. His six Space Hawks books were published in mainland China in conjunction with China's first manned space mission. His nonfiction book *Imagining the Universe,* won a *Scientific American* book award. He self-published his book *All It Takes— The Three Keys to Making Wise Decisions and Not Making Stupid Ones* in 2011. *Notes from the Afterlife* is his first novel.

.

40
XX1
122 - 4
142
6
184 7

Made in the USA
San Bernardino, CA
29 August 2013